THE LAST PAGEANT IN TEXAS

A NOVEL

Villa Sarita Publishing

[handwritten inscription]

The Last Pageant in Texas

Villa Sarita Publishing

VILLA SARITA PUBLISHING
Napa Valley, California

Copyright © 2019 by S.L. Cunningham

S.L. Cunningham/Villa Sarita Publishing
Napa Valley, California
lopezs10@live.com

Publisher's Note: This is a work of fiction. All characters, organizations, businesses, places, and events are a product of the author's imagination or are used fictitiously. Any resemblance to actual people, living or dead, or to businesses, companies, events, institutions, or locales is completely coincidental.

Ordering Information: For details, contact the publisher at the email address above.

Villa Sarita Publishing/S.L. Cunningham – First Edition

Cover art: Ladybyrd

Book Interior and E-book Design by
Amit Dey | amitdey2528@gmail.com

ISBN 978-0-578-55812-7 (pbk)
ISBN 978-0-578-55813-4 (ebook)

Printed in the United States of America

For my parents, obvi, for Danny and Cleggerator for reading first drafts, for my critique partners who helped shape this book, for Bob who helped me brainstorm a new title, for Napa Valley Writers for its constant encouragement and for those who read my first book.

Now let's party and eat brains!

CHAPTER 1

THE VERY NEAR FUTURE

Beaumont, TX

"If you were given the chance to change something from the past, what would it be?"

Dammit, that question should have gone to me. I would have answered it a *lot* better than fat-ass Bernice.

"What can be your greatest contribution to the community?"

Well, crud. Another question I could have answered perfectly. I discreetly wiped my hands on the side of my evening wear, while keeping a large smile on my makeup-caked face.

Of course, smarty-pants Ashley Carson would get this question. She would answer it perfectly and flash her pearly whites (fake) and the audience would eat it up (idiots).

"Well, Todd," Ashley said, smiling at first as she acknowledged the emcee asking the question, then the judges, before making her face somber-like because this was a serious question and serious questions weren't received warmly if you were grinning. "It's going to be difficult for me to choose just one, but I'm going to have to say the greatest environmental problem we face today is the man-made toxins that have proved to be harmful to humans and animals alike. Small gestures, such as purchasing organic food and products, are ways that we can come together as a human race to reduce the use of these pollutants."

The stupid audience clapped like crazy, even though half of them were there to support girls competing against her.

It took everything in me to keep my eyeballs from rolling back in my head, and I felt myself start to flush. Dammit, where was Celia? My stepmom had complained of not feeling well when we woke up this morning, so I let her sleep in while I got ready by my lonesome in the hotel. My turn was coming up and if she missed my moment I would be madder than a tick on a hairless hound. She was the one who recorded all my pageants, had since my first one at six months. She wasn't my favorite person, but she knew how to work an iPhone better than any pageant coach I knew.

I willed my heart to stop beating so damn fast and tried to distract myself by checking out my so-called competition. Today's pageant, Miss Biscuits & Gravy, was supposed to be one of the year's biggest events for those of us who lived and breathed sashes, butt glue and crowns high enough to poke out Jesus' cornea in heaven above. So, it was more than just a little weird that there was only a handful of contestants today, and looking out at the crowd, I noticed a lot of empty chairs, more than at other events I'd participated in.

When Celia and I first got to Wexin Hotel in Beaumont, Texas a couple of days ago from our hometown of Atlanta, Georgia, I had heard elevator chatter about a nasty flu going around but didn't pay much attention. I was used to pageants being held in hotels, but the Wexin was one of the largest airport hotels in the USA, so there was no surprise it'd be an obvious breeding pool for colds and such. Looks like it was a bad one if there were this many ladies missing. It was a shame I wouldn't be collecting my Grand Supreme prize in front of a larger audience, but as long as the sponsor of the pageant— Earl Nelson, owner of The Biscuits & Gravy Warehouse chain—was there I would make do with the situation. It was just a tad annoying that Celia, whose obsession with pageants ran deeper than mine, still wasn't here. It was totally unlike her, even if she was sick, and I didn't know if I should be worried or pissed.

"Kat, *Gawd,* pay some frickin attention," whispered a voice behind me.

I jumped and realized that Todd, the emcee, had been calling my name. I felt my cheeks turn pink and then red when I heard laughter behind me. I took a quick breath, tossed my extension-laden brunette tresses away from my shoulders, and put on my show face. I smiled brightly as I pranced confidently toward the middle of the stage.

"Well, Katherine Abbott, that was some deep thought you were in!" drawled Todd, winking in an exaggerated manner toward the crowd. "What could a pretty thing like you be thinking so hard about?" He grinned at the audience, and they played right along, giggling at my expense.

Ugh, what a douchebag.

I laughed lightly to show the judges I was a good sport. "Todd, before I go on stage, I give a little prayer for thanks of all of my wonderful peers. I guess y'all caught me off guard a bit!"

The onlookers sighed in appreciation, and Todd softened his expression. "Well, darlin', ain't that precious! Okay, let's get on to your question." He pulled a card from the stack in his hands. "Here we go. Katherine, what do you think has been the most important discovery during your lifetime?"

I mentally high-fived myself. This was going to be easy-peasy. I opened my mouth, then shut it as the conference room door flung open, slamming against the wall. Everyone turned to look, and I glared against the light to see who was trying to take away attention from my moment. I stepped forward out of the spotlight to get a better look. A woman with crazy, Einstein-with-bed-head hair was crawling jerkily down the aisle on her hands and feet like some sort of animal. She stopped right in front of the sound table and lifted her head up as if sniffing the air. I felt my throat close when she stopped and stared directly at me. Even with the lights shining in my eyes, I knew who she was. Even with her leg bent crooked like it was broken—and even though she was in what looked like a soiled nightgown—I knew it was Celia.

I stood frozen.

I heard chatter all around me as my stepmother crouched. This certainly wasn't the first time a drunk pageant mom tried to steal the limelight, and it certainly wouldn't be the last. I simply couldn't believe it was mine, acting like this freak show in front of everybody. This was the same lady who woke up an hour before my daddy did, just to put her makeup on. Something was going on, but I was too mortified to do anything other than stare.

Todd pushed me aside and hopped down from the stage, puffing his chest out like he was ten times bigger than his slender frame actually was. "Now look here, Ma'am, this here is a private event and you can't…" He stopped talking as he got closer to Celia. Todd looked down at her and let out a shriek. He clumsily tried to back-pedal, putting his hands in front of his face.

Celia let out a horrifying squeal and sprang toward Todd, smashing him to the floor. Her head bounced up and down like she was initiating a lewd act, but the spray of blood spurting from his neck said differently.

Those closest to them began to scream. Within seconds, the entire audience was in full panic, charging towards the exit doors, not caring if they were mowing down kids in sparkly dresses who were moving too slowly. Chairs toppled over, and I stared in horror as people trampled over family members, climbing over moving bodies to some presumed safety.

The girls backstage scattered, running to get away from the room—away from me. Some of them were crying; others had full-blown terror streaked across their faces as they violently pushed past each other to get away.

None of this made any sense. I stood, willing myself to move away, but I just couldn't understand what the hell was happening. I forced my laden feet to head tentatively toward the front of the stage, in Celia's direction.

I stopped and hesitated as I stared. Maybe it wasn't my stepmom. Maybe I thought it was because I had been thinking about her.

But... but maybe it actually was Celia, and here I was acting like a selfish fool and she needed my help, and what the hell was I doing staring like she wasn't my almost blood?

I took a second step forward and felt relief sweep across my body. Yes, I would help, and everything would be all right. I just needed to get down off the stage, and this would all be explained away by dinner tonight, and we would eventually laugh about this, and it would become this crazy inside joke, and no one in the pageant world would judge me because obviously Celia was sick, and maybe she had accidentally touched a wild animal, like a beaver, or... or a raccoon. Everyone knew those critters carried disease like pink on a hog.

I ignored the inner voice screaming at me that I was wrong, and continued to walk ahead with false bravado.

I was almost off stage when someone ran in front of me, grabbed me and threw me over their shoulder before bolting towards the doors.

I opened my mouth to scream—and locked eyes with Celia, who was now smeared in red. She stared back at me, and her lips lifted into a lopsided, manic grin.

Before I could call out, she broke eye contact and lowered her head, burying her mouth into Todd's limp body.

My vision became fuzzy and my lips grew numb.

Then, there was nothing but black.

CHAPTER 2

"**H**mmm, did I win?" My voice sounded thick and lazy. I blinked, not understanding why I was no longer on stage.

"Okay, Bernice, back up. Give her some air."

I blinked again and winced. Bright sunshine pierced my eyeballs.

"Hold up, Kat. I'm pretty sure you're in shock. Just sit for a minute, okay?"

I squinted against the sun to see who was talking to me like I was an idiot.

"Porker? Porker Schroeder? What are YOU doing here?" I rubbed my eyes as my brain struggled to make sense. Why was I lying on the ground, and why was I outside? Why was the biggest red-headed nerd from my high school kneeling by me like we were amigos? And why was fat-ass Bernice staring at me like I had grown two heads?

"Oh, God—CELIA!" I sat violently upright and felt the earth spin around me.

"It's Parker, *not* Porker, and I guess a thank you for saving your life from a lunatic is out of the question," muttered the chubby boy.

I ignored him and pushed myself up, feeling trapped in what felt like a silk taffeta straitjacket. My chest began to constrict, and my brain screamed at my body that now wasn't the time for a panic attack. I furiously slapped loose asphalt, leaves and Lord knew what else from my hair, then tore off my dress until I was down to just a strapless bra and a pair of Spanx. Porker turned away, his cheeks red. Normally I would have never disrobed so publicly, but I was sure I would have passed out again if I had kept that skin-tight torture device on my body one second longer. The fact that it was a million degrees outside made my decision to strip that much easier.

I took in a breath and gagged. Oh heavens, it smelled horrible. I covered my mouth and looked around, realizing I was behind a row of dumpsters that had been baking in the Texas heat like gumbo trash.

"You have to be kidding me. Why are we even out here? And who the hell picked this place?" I kept my nose covered, waving my other hand in front of me.

"You seriously don't remember? My brother *saved* you. You could have been just like Todd." Bernice stuck her stout hand on her equally stout waist, glaring at me.

I wasn't listening. Frankly, I didn't care why I was back here, or why Porker decided to carry me out like he was a poor man's superhero. All I could think about, all I could mentally *see* was that hotel conference room where the pageant was happening and what I think I saw my stepmother do. I needed to go back. I needed to see if there was any chance in hell that Celia might not have been as bad as what I was picturing. If there was even a small chance she was just feverish or along the lines, then I was going to get her to the nearest hospital ASAP.

My heels were the first thing I took off before peeking around the dumpster, straining until I caught sight of the hotel. Which now looked like it was on fire.

Great.

Porker grabbed my arm as I started to walk toward the hotel, surprising me with his agility. He looked pissed off, still gripping me as I tried to throw off his hand.

"Are you crazy?" he asked angrily. "You can't go back in there! That lady in there wasn't the only one who was eating people's faces. We musta' passed about a dozen others just like her before we found this hiding place." He paused and noticed my blank stare. Then he started to speak again, this time a bit more gently. "Kat, I think we're lucky we're even *alive*. We need to find a car and we need to get somewhere safe. Do you understand? That lady could have killed you!"

"That lady? That *lady*? That lady happens to be my *stepmother*, you asshole!"

"That was Mrs. Abbott?"

Porker and I both turned towards the shaky voice.

"I'm so sorry, Kat... I didn't recognize her." Bernice looked at me, her eyes swollen and red. I looked down and noticed she was holding Porker's hand.

Brother and sister. Fat and fatter. Twins as a matter of fact. Porker must be here to chaperone while she tried (pathetically) to vie for a pageant title. I rarely had time to hang out with people from school, and even if I did, it wouldn't have been with those two losers. Porker was the kind of guy who played Dungeons and Dragons at lunch while Bernice spent her time tutoring. Word was they were both going to graduate a year early. Which meant I would get one more year of high school without wondering how two people could eat as many calories in a day as they probably did without having a heart attack.

I stared at Bernice until she looked away. I didn't need sympathy—and I certainly didn't need it from someone with multiple chins.

"I couldn't give two hoots about your ratchet reasoning. If that's where Celia is then I'm going in there *now*. You can't stop me, you hear?" I straightened my shoulders, hating that I was wasting time.

Porker stared at me, while Bernice unsuccessfully sniffed back tears.

"Okay," he said slowly. "Okay, fine. Go back in there. But don't say I didn't warn you."

He didn't know what he was talking about. So, a few people were sick and acting weird. Who cared? I was better off without these two.

I pirouetted as if I was back on stage and walked away from the dumpsters.

I stopped, not even getting ten feet.

In less than an hour, the city of Beaumont had gone from Texas normalcy to looking like a war zone on CNN. Apart from the hotel enveloped in a plume of smoke and flames, I was shaken to see injured people lying on the street, while others streaked by me. Store windows were shattered, with frantic people running out holding whatever they could carry. Helicopters flew deafeningly loud overhead, dipping dangerously low enough for me to feel a breeze.

A loud metallic crash made me jump, then look over my shoulder in fear. A news van had smashed into a tree. The door flew open, releasing a cloud of dark smoke. The van rocked a bit, then was still. A high-heel shoe with a torn foot still inside flew out, smacking me in the chest. All I could do was stare while the stump pulsated blood onto my Spanx.

Before I could mentally recover, someone pushed into me and I turned, holding my hand to my mouth to keep from screaming.

A woman, only a few years older than me, stood in front of me, her eyes vacant, with half of her face melting like candle wax. She reeked of burning meat. "Do you know when the shuttle leaves?" she mumbled. "I need to find my husband. Do you know when the shuttle leaves?" She stumbled off. She was naked, except for a pair of torn panties that read "Sunday" on the back. I was now paralyzed with pure fear. Even if I had gone after her I wouldn't have known how to help.

I didn't notice the boy until it was too late. He sprang past me, running on his hands and feet until he flung himself onto the woman.

She didn't even scream as he began to bite at her stomach, ripping chunks of flesh from her body as she lay looking at the sky, her foot shaking with the boy's movements. Her head turned toward mine, and for a moment our eyes connected.

I fell to my knees and pitched forward, the world becoming out of focus, yet again. I needed to go home. I needed to find Celia. I needed…

I felt Porker before I saw him. Yet again, the person I ignored every day in school was coming to my rescue.

"We go to the hotel and grab what we need, and then we are *leaving*. Nod if you understand."

I nodded and clutched his hand, feeling nearly high from the touch of a familiar person.

He helped me to my feet, and I noticed Bernice following close behind.

"Okay, guys, stay next to each other and be on the lookout. We have ten minutes and then we're outta' here." Porker motioned with his hand. "It's about suppertime and the light's fading fast. Look for flashlights and such. We're going to need them."

Porker's voice was a million miles away. I couldn't think of flashlights when I was able to taste the burnt meat of that woman's skin. My stomach turned like a flapjack. I shook my head, trying to get the image of her looking at me, looking *through* me, out of my mind.

Bernice grabbed my hand, breaking my memory with her clamminess.

We got to the front of the hotel lobby doors where just yesterday a cute porter had helped Celia and me with our luggage.

"Shit!" said Porker, as we looked inside.

Shit was right. Smoke filled the hotel, allowing us to only see a few feet ahead. This wasn't good.

"We only have time to go to a couple hotel rooms, and if I've learned anything from horror films, we are *not* splitting up, so we should link arms. Even though the power's out, the rooms will still be locked. Our key cards most likely won't work, even if I knew where ours was. We'll just have to hope some random room doors didn't close all the way so we can go in and grab anything you think will be useful." Porker turned to Bernice, who was trembling so much her fat cheeks wobbled. "Stick by me, okay, Sissy? Nothing will happen to you, but you *need* to stay by me."

He pushed open the door after motioning to us to cover our faces from the smoke.

We crept into the lobby, which was still full of frantic folk. I couldn't tell who was normal and who wasn't. The front desk looked abandoned, and I noticed the outline of a fire extinguisher on the wall. I nudged Porker and he nodded at me. We headed towards it.

He grabbed the extinguisher and we started making our way to the first-floor hotel rooms. I knew Porker had said we shouldn't split up, and out loud I had agreed with him, but really, I wasn't here for them. I was here to save Celia and myself, no one else.

I pulled my hand away. "I'll meet you guys outside," I lied, leaning into Porker so he could hear me properly.

"Dammit, Kat, why are you making this harder than it needs to be? I told you already—we can't split up!"

We looked at each, neither of us wanting to give in first.

I knew I didn't have time to play "mine is bigger than yours." I decided to be honest because I knew one way or another I was getting back to the auditorium, where the pageant had just been.

"You know where I'm heading. You can stay here, grabbing shampoo bottles and whatever else, or you can come with." I held my chin up. I knew I could go alone, but Lord help me, I really didn't want to. I didn't know what I would find—as much as I was telling myself that Celia wouldn't attack me, I had a weird feeling deep in my gut.

"Okay," he said, with only a second of hesitation. "Let's go."

Utter relief flushed my body. I nodded my thanks and headed to my destination, the twins following close behind.

As I was opening the room's heavy door, it dawned on me that I might be putting us all in extreme danger.

I shrugged it off and straightened my shoulders. Now was not the time to think like a pansy. I came here for one reason and one reason only.

I was here to get my stepmother and get the *hell* out of Texas.

CHAPTER 3

A part of me knew I had been lying to myself. I knew I came across as a no-bullshit, take-no-prisoners type of gal. I was aware I had an "intimidating" presence as my school counselor liked to say. When I had decided to walk back inside the hotel, I told myself that maybe Celia was fine. Maybe it wasn't so bad. Maybe Todd was still alive, bitching about how the fluorescent lighting made his t-zone too shiny.

I let my hand linger on the heavy door. There was still an option to chicken out. Maybe the police were already on their way and they could deal with this. But what if they weren't? And I was Celia's only hope? God, I couldn't believe this was really happening. Just a few hours earlier, my biggest dilemma was choosing between a Maybelline or Cover Girl lipstick.

The twins breathing down my neck created a temporary feeling of heroism and I pushed the door open.

It was too dark inside, or at least dark enough to make me take a small step back. The remaining sunlight coming in from the lobby cast horrible shadows across the floor and stage. My fingers found the light switch, but it was soon apparent the power was out. I let my eyes struggle to adjust as I scanned the room, looking for movement.

I spied closed curtains against a large window and motioned that I was going over. Porker tightened his grip on my arm, and we crept forward.

We shuffled as silently as we could while making the seemingly never-ending trip.

"Ouch!" I stumbled, catching myself just as I was about to fall.

"What's wrong?" he whispered as he froze, staring wildly around me.

I motioned to my foot. "Sorry... I wasn't paying attention and I tripped. Damn, that hurt!" I kept my voice low, but my words must have carried because Bernice's blotchy face appeared from the dark as she slinked close by her brother.

"What's going on?" She looked fearfully at Porker.

"Shhh, Sissy, it's fine. Kat just tripped on something. Probably a table leg. I'm going to open the curtains and you just stay put. I'll be right back, okay?"

Bernice hesitated, then nodded slowly. Her brown eyes filled with tears, and her nose began to drip. It took everything in me to not show how disgusted I was with her. It was *my* stepmom who had been chewing on the pageant host like trail mix, not hers.

I gave Porker a tight smile, but he had already started to walk toward the curtains. He reached one end and pulled slowly.

Sunlight flooded the first half of the room. We paused, all of us tense as our eyes roamed around.

My skin grew cold as I stared at the turned-over chairs and tables and at the ripped-up carpet. Abandoned shoes, purses and even a few wigs littered the floor. Goose pimples rose up and down my body as I wrapped my arms around myself.

I heard Porker grunt as he pulled on the second curtain.

I threw a hand up to cover my eyes and stepped backward, falling over whatever the hell my foot had come in contact with before.

Holy heck, that smarted! I still wasn't wearing any shoes (a problem I would need to solve ASAP), so anything my now-ruined pedicure touched hurt like the dickens.

I looked down and gasped.

Todd's head, or what was left of it, stared up at my lady parts. His chunky blond highlights were smeared dark red and his left cheek was nothing but a jagged hole showing me a glimpse of bleached-white molars.

Bernice let out a strangled scream. I whipped around, putting a finger to my lips to get her to shut her trap.

The hair on my arms rose as I saw Bernice wasn't looking at Todd.

She wasn't even looking at me.

She was looking behind me.

"Don't. Move." Porker's face drained of color as he saw what Bernice was looking at.

I froze, watching Porker inch his way over while keeping a wide-eyed stare at whatever was behind me.

I couldn't take standing around like a sitting duck any longer.

I gulped and tightened my stomach in as I turned around.

Something that resembled Celia was now in front of me, sitting on her haunches like an animal. Her hair was matted in what I knew was blood. She reeked of death, and her eyes were a bright red that locked onto mine as she stared into my face.

She tilted her head catawampus-like, still staring. For a moment, she looked so much like the stepmother that I had just left in the hotel room that I reached out my hand to touch her.

"NO!"

Porker was beside me in a second (seriously, *how* did he move so fast with all of that extra weight?) and pushed my hand down just as Celia lunged forward, her mouth open with an angry hunger in her eyes. He pushed me toward Bernice while grabbing a chair, frantically waving and pushing it around in the air.

A loud clamor by the stage stopped all of us. My head snapped to the left, only to see the runner-up's trophy on the floor in glittered bits and pieces.

"Are you... are you one of *them*?" came a faint voice from behind the trophy table.

Celia turned her head and sniffed the air. She locked on to the table and sprinted on all fours, with her belly low to the ground.

"Run!" hollered Bernice. "Whoever's behind there, you need to run!"

The table flipped over and a blur of pink and blonde hair leaped from behind, running to Bernice's voice. Bernice grabbed the yellow-tressed survivor and they both headed to the door, back into the lobby.

Porker grasped the chair and swung as Celia changed direction and charged back toward us.

The chair smashed into my stepmom's nose. She let out a whimper and crashed to the floor. She lay there, seemingly dazed, then shook her head, regaining her consciousness.

Celia bared her teeth and hissed. She tensed, and it reminded me of when my old dog, Charlie, would growl at our mailman.

Charlie hated him with every bone in his body.

My stepmother was looking at me with the same hatred.

I knew now, as clear as a June sky, that this thing in front of me was a monster—and Celia was gone.

As the Creature-Formally-Known-As-Celia lunged for my neck, I grabbed the closest thing on the table next to us and aimed it toward her.

A sure and steady stream of Aqua Net blasted into the thing's face. It screeched and choked as it gagged and waved its hands against the sticky cloud. If there was any doubt that my stepmother was on her way out, this was it. Celia of all people would have known that hairspray was a friend, and never a foe. She fell backward onto the prizewinner's table, not noticing the winner's trophy beneath her. She was still struggling as the trophy pierced through the back of her skull and out her forehead. Her body gave one last shudder before growing still.

"Is it... is *she* dead?" I whispered. I couldn't feel my fingers or toes. Celia had always been more a hardened coach than a mother figure to me, but she was still family.

"It wasn't her, Kat. It was something else. A demon, I don't know. But it wasn't her. We need to get out of here. Come on." Porker gently took my hand, leading me out of the room.

I couldn't tell if my face was wet from my former stepmother's blood or from the tears streaming down my cheeks.

CHAPTER 4

"**H**oly shit," wheezed Porker, catching up to his sister and the shaking, bubblegum-pink-ballroom-gowned person she had rescued. The two were huddled out by the auditorium doors, but I could barely make them out from the heavy smoke that surrounded us. "Are you guys okay?"

What?! Were THEY okay? What about me?

I stared blankly at the boy who I knew saw the same thing I just did, which proved I really wasn't going crazy. I just witnessed my stepmother take her first steps to the pearly gates. And I think I helped do it. If I hadn't used that Aqua Net, maybe Celia would still be alive.

"Kat, thank you, thank you," gasped a velvety voice from the smoky air.

Ashley Carson, my lifelong pageant nemesis, owner of a stomach flatter than a Monopoly board, and supposed "high-fashion model in Japan," limped our way, holding on to an ever-sniffling Bernice.

"You legit just saved my life! If you hadn't thought to use that hairspray, I for sure would be a goner!"

I turned my stare to Ashley and heard the rage pulse in my eardrums as I realized that the pink-dressed blonde who had been hiding behind the trophy table was none other than the fakest, most plastic harlot of my high school. I had known Ashley my whole life, from school and from the pageant circle, and she had been a thorn in my side since day one. *She* was the one who had made that noise, which had made my stepmother/ the creature attack. That mother fu—

"Ashley!" I said, forcing something that resembled a smile onto my face. "How nice to see you... alive."

Ashley was oblivious to my tone of voice. Or she chose to ignore it.

"What in tarnation is even happening? I was knocked out by that stampede on stage, and next thing I know there's smoke and fire and something's running after me. And God, all this noise!" Her face drained and she grabbed at Porker. "Oh, my Lord, is it terrorists? Is that what this is?"

Porker laid a hand on Ashley's shoulder, softening his face.

I rolled my eyes. Males were always suckers for her baby blues and shiny blonde hair. The fact that she was built like a lingerie brand ambassador didn't hurt either. She was easily the most popular girl in our school, despite being a junior like the twins and me. I could have been just as popular if Celia had let me have friends, but when you're working to become the youngest Miss America on record, it didn't allow for much free time.

"It could be. That was actually one of the first things I also thought of," admitted Porker, while discreetly trying to suck in his stomach. "It would make sense because the media has been warning us of an airborne chemical attack for years." He frowned and looked around. "The only problem with that theory is, why Beaumont? Why not a larger city that would make more of an impact?"

"Oh my God, who cares? I thought we were trying to get somewhere safe. You know, so we don't *die*." I didn't bother to hide my sarcasm.

"Good thinking, Kat," said Ashley, turning her sympathetic face to me. "I don't want to be a burden, but I really need to call my parents. What did yours say when you called? I bet they were freaking out like crazy!"

I had been so swept up with finding and then losing my stepmom that I hadn't even thought of calling my dad. Oh no, no, no! He must have been calling Celia or me and was probably out of his head with worry!

"Uh, that was Mrs. Abbott that was... um, you know, that was hunting you down," whispered Bernice with the subtle tone of a foghorn.

"Oh, Lord, oh, Kat, I didn't know!" Ashley threw her hand over her mouth and her eyes filled with delicate tears. She started toward me, her arms open.

Please tell me she isn't trying to hug me.

I stepped just outside of her embrace and walked to where I thought I remembered the stairs were. I knew I was being rude, but I didn't care. Ashley was putting on an act and I could see right through her. I had acted in a similar fashion in the past and knew her game too well. I needed to walk away before I said or did something regrettable.

"Kat! Where the hell do you think you're going?" Porker asked. His voice had an assertive tone, and I knew it was probably because he wanted to show Ashley that he was "in charge."

"You said we need supplies," I said over my shoulder, not stopping. "You get them your way, and I'll get them mine. I'm heading upstairs to see if my room will open."

"You won't be able to see. It's gotta be pitch black in there. Here, take my phone." Porker was already turning the light on his cell to hand to me.

I grabbed it, mumbling a thank you. He hadn't even called his family, and he was letting me use his phone as a flashlight, ignoring the fact that I was being a little bit of a brat.

Porker started to say something else, and I knew I had to say something first before he convinced me to stay with them.

"I know you don't want us to split up. But I know where I'm going and I'll be fine. I'll meet y'all down here in fifteen and we'll get to some sort of safety. Right now, I need you to not argue with me because, frankly, you're just wasting time."

"Let her go," said Ashley. Her gentle voice made me want to gag. "Kat's strong, she'll be okay."

Of course, Ashley wanted me to leave. She was probably hoping I would get attacked so *she* could be the prettiest one of the group.

Bitch.

Hot liquid pulsed behind my pupils, and I furiously stomped ahead. I squinted to see better, searching for the door to the stairs. My searching hands found it before my eyes did. I pulled it open, then slammed it hard.

The smoke in the stairwell wasn't as heavy as it was in the lobby, but I was on high alert, especially as I realized, like a moron, that I had nothing to protect myself. I looked down at the phone's feeble glow, and sighed. Crud! I forgot for a hot second I didn't even have proper attire on. Too bad I couldn't use my bra as a weapon. That stupid underwire had impaled me enough times in the past. Now, it was more worthless than hen shit on a pump handle.

I wiped the hair from my face and began climbing the stairs. Of course, Celia had insisted on an eighth-floor room. Lucky for me, she had also insisted on daily cardio to maintain my figure, so the trip up wouldn't be that hard.

I started cautiously, as I couldn't see squat, and by the third floor I was taking two steps at a time. My heart raced, and I felt my head clear as endorphins flooded my body, forcing the fear of the unknown at bay. At least for now. In the moment, it almost felt like things were back to normal. Almost like this was just a regular workout session with the trainer I'd had since hitting puberty.

I reached my floor in good time and calmed my breathing before pressing my ear to the hallway door. It was radio-silent. For some reason, that scared me more than if I had heard shouting and explosions.

Like a cautious kid putting one toe in a pool, I slowly opened the door and peeked out, the light from the phone barely illuminating the floor. I *really* wished I had thought to bring that damn fire extinguisher.

The windows at the end of each hall gave off enough fading light for me to see there was nothing lurking in the hallway. I opened the door all the way and stepped out onto the floor. I threw myself against the closest wall and tentatively began my journey to Room 827.

All was still until I reached Room 814. I crept forward and my heartbeat quickened when I saw that the door had been ripped off its hinges and was covered in deep scratch marks. Inside, I could hear grunting, but couldn't tell if it was human or—or a creature like my stepmother.

Jesus Christ, please feel free to stop focusing on, like, Haiti, and give me a little attention down here.

My breathing sped up and my head became woozy as I tried to figure out what to do. I had two basic options. One, run as fast as I could to my room and hope it didn't draw in whatever evil was lurking on the floor. Two, see what was inside Room 814.

I knew which choice made the most sense, but for some reason I wasn't feeling too right in the head. I guess seeing your stepmother smashed with a chair like a wrestling champion will do that to you.

My false bravado pumped enough adrenaline for me to creep toward the room. A piece of wood sticking out of the door caught my attention, and I worked it free until I had something sharp enough to do damage with.

I took a long lunge forward while keeping my pitiful wood dagger in front of me. If I had watched nerdy shows like *Game of Thrones* instead of *Real Housewives* I probably would have a better idea on how to actually fight. Whenever things went back to normal, I was *so* going to switch up my DVR.

My foot landed in a squishy warm pile. Gagging, I pulled it away quickly, but not quick enough to see where I was stepping next. My other foot slammed onto something slick and slimy, and I stumbled around before grabbing onto a nearby table.

Ewwwww… so gross.

"Help… me," whispered a voice by where I had just stepped.

I clasped my stake and followed the voice to a figure crumpled on the ground.

"Help," he gurgled. "Hurts."

"Shhhh!" I whispered. "You need to stay quiet, mister. I'm coming over, hold on."

I nervously looked around to see if we had attracted any unwelcome company. It was still quiet, which was freaky and unsettling. I was hoping the grunting had come from this guy, and not a group of hungry freaks waiting to announce themselves at any second. What I wouldn't give for a scream in the hallway to let me know there were others alive.

I crouched down, taking one last sweep of the room before looking at the man in front of me. He was Asian, dressed in what looked like an expensive business suit, and he was whiter than my uncle Barry's legs during winter.

He grabbed my hand and I recoiled at his cold touch.

"Need... police. Need... 911." He closed his eyes in pain and pointed to his stomach.

I let go of his hand and scrambled backward. How the HELL was he alive? His stomach looked like it had been turned inside out, and as I followed the intestine trail, I now knew what I had stepped on earlier.

His head turned slightly so he could meet my eyes.

We stared at each other while blood pooled between us.

He started to cough violently, and a warm red spray hit my face.

I reached for him and desperately put my hands over his open body, trying to do something, anything, to help. My palms moved with each chest spasm, feeling more helpless with every movement he made. He shuddered and weakly moved my arms aside.

"You... leave." He coughed feebly. "No help. No... good. Just... leave."

Oh, what a shit day this was.

If there had been a chance I was Heaven bound, it no longer existed. I stood up and turned, leaving the dying man alone.

It's what he wanted. You're just doing what he asked. You aren't a bad person.

Nothing I told myself made me feel like I had done the right thing, but time was running out. Clenching my jaw, I walked out of his room, dragging my feet until I found 827. I reached for the handle.

Locked. Of course.

I studied my options. One, try another room and hope the previous occupant had brought cute clothes. Or two, tap into my inner Jason Statham and find something heavy enough to break the handle off. Considering my best Rachel Zoe tank was inside, I chose the latter.

Quickly settling on finding something of use in the turned-over housekeeping cart, I rummaged through the side bins and curled my hand around a metal canister of furniture polish. I quietly ran back to my room, giving a quick prayer to Mr. Clean that the noise wouldn't attract any hungry freaks. I raised my arm and brought it down hard, smashing it against what I was hoping was the weak part of the handle. Six tries later, I was in, albeit with a throbbing shoulder.

Inside, time stood still. My flat iron was still plugged in and the room smelled like Celia's signature perfume—Faith Hill's Soul 2 Soul. I looked at the bed I had slept in so peacefully the night before, and wanted nothing more than to crawl under the duvet and wait for someone to tell me everything was okay.

The sight of my blood-splattered face in the wall mirror slapped me back to reality. This was really happening. My stepmom was dead and I was stuck with a group of people I couldn't stand. Maybe I had already died and this was Hell. I looked closer in the mirror. Yes, maybe I died back in the lobby. Only in Hell would my skin look so dry and my hair this greasy.

I could feel the blood tightening on my skin as it dried. I needed to clean up. I didn't want a constant reminder of what—who—I had just walked away from.

No water came from the bathroom sink. Or the shower. I looked around, before resting my eyes on the latrine.

I sighed.

Celia had been big on fiber, so the chances she had crapped before going ape-shit crazy were high. I tried not to think about it as I gingerly flipped the toilet seat up and stuck a towel in the water, rubbing it on my cheeks. After scrubbing as much of my body as I could reach, I walked back inside the room. For the first time in my life, I avoided the other mirrors.

My Spanx went straight into the garbage after wrestling with them to come off. I threw on my Rachel Zoe and the first pair of jeans and shoes I could find and stuffed my pockets with essentials. On my way out, I grabbed my phone and charger. Calling my dad was a priority, but now wasn't the time.

I closed the door behind me and avoided looking into room 814 as I ran down the hall.

That was my first mistake.

My toothbrush fell from my pocket, and I slowed down as I went to grab it.

That was my second mistake.

A loud hissing echoed in the hall.

The dying businessman that I had felt so awful for leaving was crouched outside his door. He cocked his head to the side, sniffing the air like Celia had done. His eyes fell on mine as they had before, but this time his eyes were bright red. Even from far away I could see his hunger. He started my way, his open gut dropping small organs on the tacky hotel carpet like a human piñata.

This made about as much sense as a screen door on a submarine, but today had taught me that when you see a crouching, red-eyed demon, even one dressed in an Armani suit, you run and you run hard.

I threw the toothbrush at the creature that was now coming at me with a galloping speed.

Flinging the hallway door open, I flew down each flight in blind panic. In an act of final desperation, I turned, slinging Porker's phone in the thing's direction. I could hear scuttling behind me as the blood-lustful thing scrambled to keep up.

My feet wouldn't stop, and I kept running, totally visionless, until I smacked into something solid. The first-floor door, finally! It opened up without me touching the knob and I stumbled forward.

"Argh!" I screamed, making a fist to defend myself.

"Kat, it's me!" Porker's eyes popped when he saw what was behind me. "Oh, shit!"

"Run, you dolt, run!" I bolted to the exit. We slammed into the lobby's revolving door with Bernice and Ashley barely squeezing into our section. The businessman and another creature crashed into the other side. Their mouths gnashed and gnawed at the glass between us, getting more and more delirious with ferocious hunger.

"I don't know what to do!" said Porker. He looked at us, frantic. "If we push this forward to get outside, those things will get out too."

Ashley and Bernice clung to each other, their faces reflecting identical sheer hysteria.

The separating glass began to crack as they continued to try and get to us.

This was it. This was the end. I was going to die a virgin. Porker was *definitely* going to die a virgin. Ashley—well, I had heard enough stories about her to know that wasn't going to be a problem of hers.

A tapping outside made us turn around. A small person dressed head to toe in all black, like a ninja, stood outside and waved. He motioned for us to come out our part of the door.

Just then, the glass began to break into chunks, forcing a decision from the four of us. We shoved the door open and were barely outside before the ninja threw something into the monsters' section of the swinging door. Firecrackers exploded and the creatures screamed in outrage.

Revving around the corner, a black SUV screeched to a halt in front of us.

"Get in!" hollered a grown woman's voice from inside.

I didn't know if it was Southern manners in respecting an adult's command or the fact that the hotel was crawling with things that wanted to eat us—but in the moment "stranger danger" didn't exist.

We obliged instantly, the ninja following close behind.

CHAPTER 5

"**H**onestly, are y'all messing with me? What the *hell* are those things?" Ashley leaned forward, breathing heavily while a worried Bernice rubbed her back.

"Honey, I don't know, but you sure are lucky that Monique here saved yo' cute butts. You weren't but a moment away from turning into The Last Supper!"

The woman driving turned around and flashed a huge smile at us. "The name is Cookie. Don't worry none, my Caddy has survived floods and break-ins and still comes back swinging."

"Who's Caddy?" Bernice asked.

"Apparently, it's short for Cadillac," answered a voice from the back.

We spun around, unaware until now that there was a whole extra row of seats behind us. Three other people were uncomfortably crammed together, watching us. I became conscious of how sweaty I was and how I probably reeked like an old Converse. I felt myself turn pink as the thin man who had answered Bernice moved his head, as if trying not to smell us directly.

"I'm Robert, and this is my daughter, Lucy." A man covered in soot pointed to himself, then to an angsty tween beside him. She scowled her hello at us, then went back to her phone. I don't know what she was so pissed at. I mean, in the old world—from just a few hours ago—Lucy would have been a four at best. Now, with the world probably depleting itself of so many people, she might have a chance at becoming a new-world six. Which would make me a fourteen, but who's counting. "We were getting ready for a friend's wedding when the fire alarm went off. If I had known it wasn't a drill…" He cleared his throat. "I lost track of my wife, Basil, trying to get Lucy to safety. The last time I saw her, she was putting on her dress." He laughed harshly. "She was wearing this ridiculous underwear I got her as a gag gift. I don't even think they said the right day on them."

Oh Jesus. What were the damn chances? I totally understood Lucy's raging expression. I opened my mouth, then closed it when Porker grabbed my thigh. I recognized it immediately as a "Shut the eff up and don't tell the poor man you saw his wife get inhaled earlier today by a boy younger than his already-mad-at-the-world daughter."

"And I'm Bernholdt," said the thin man sitting on the other side. "I was on my way to a Jack London symposium. I was actually on the plane when I was bitten by a horribly rowdy child. I apparently hit him a little too hard and airport security forced me off." He sniffed. "That's the last time I ever book a flight on an economy website. Now I'm stuck in this dump of a city while my fellow scholars enjoy talks of *The Iron Heel*."

"Nice to meet everyone. Sorry, I'm not at my best." Ashley looked up and gave a brave smile to those in the back.

Without looking, I knew they all fell in love with her. The fact that she was still in her pageant wear made her look like a fairytale princess in need of saving. She was so full of shit her eyes should be brown, yet folks threw themselves all over each other for just a minute of her attention. I became more aware of how cruddy I looked. I was used to being the one who made jaws drop. Now, it felt like even Porker was scooting away from me.

"Wait, you were bit?" Porker turned to Bernholdt who held his arm out in proof.

"Barf," said the tween, rolling her eyes. She crossed her arms, glowering at her dad.

"Honey, Cookie will look after you. Cookie will look afta' all of you," boomed the voice up front. "First, we need to get some food in you! Second, we gonna get you newbies washed up!"

I didn't know where we were going, who the hell Cookie was or why the ninja up front wasn't speaking. But I was tired and hungry, and the thought of getting clean sounded divine. She looked like a nice enough lady and, besides, if she tried any funny business I would just shove one of the others at her for a distraction.

We drove in silence. Outside, the air was smoky and mute, highlighting the lack of fauna. I had done pageants all over Texas and I knew you couldn't go anywhere without the audible screams of ten million cicadas. The stillness gave me chills as my brain began to create far-fetched scenarios of what had happened to all the animals and bugs.

A vibration in my pocket startled me back to reality. I scrambled to grab my phone before the call went to voicemail.

"Hello? Daddy, can you hear me?"

"Kat, sweetheart, are you okay? I've been sick with worry! Are you with Celia? I've been calling you two and calling the hotel since this morning and no one's picking up! What's going on?"

Hearing my dad's familiar voice was like the smell of lasagna during a Weight Watchers meeting. Pure happiness followed by sickening reality.

"There's all sorts of crazy news—nothing is telling it straight! First, I hear some virus has taken over Beaumont. Then I'm starting to hear it's been reported in a few other cities. Hell, local TV reported it's even happening in Germany! Neil from across the street says it has to be ISIS, but then Mary—you remember Mary don't you, from the diner—said she heard from her sister's ex-husband's niece that Iraq is practically gone and no one can get ahold of any officials..." He stopped and gave an embarrassed laugh. "I'm sorry, hon, I'm just rambling like I always do when I'm uneasy. I'm just so glad I finally get to hear your voice." His voice broke, mirroring how my heart was currently feeling.

"Daddy," I said, closing my eyes to shut out everyone looking at me. "I have something to tell you." I heard the anxiety in my voice and I hated that all these folks were here during this conversation. I couldn't believe I had to tell him about Celia, in a car full of eavesdropping strangers no less.

Bernice placed her hand on my shoulder, which I quickly shrugged off.

"I, uh, I lost Celia."

Silence radiated through the car and over the phone.

"I don't think I'm following you," said my dad after a few seconds. "Can't you use that fancy app, that one that tracks down people from their phone?"

Dear God, he was making this hard. My throat was clogging fast with an invisible ball of emotions I didn't want to be feeling. Lord forgive me, but I knew I wasn't strong enough to continue.

"Yeah, uh, wow, I should of thought of that. I'll let you know if—when I find her."

My dad's relief was almost pitiful. Celia had always worn the pants in our family. Daddy was the one most likely to cry at a Kleenex commercial while my stepmother once got bit on the thumb by a rattler, sucked out most of the poison and continued on with her day like it wasn't nothing more than a mosquito bite. He wouldn't be able to continue, knowing that the matriarch of our family had met her demise in a hotel auditorium with outdated carpeting.

"I heard the airport is still open. I'm booking flights for you two now. Just get there as quickly as you can, okay?"

We said our goodbyes, with me promising to call him back soon with a stepmother that no longer existed.

Nobody acknowledged my lie, which I was more grateful for than I would ever let on. I should have said right then and there that I needed to head to the airport—but I kept quiet. I wanted some time to recharge, and time to think of what falsehood I would need to tell my father next.

"Kat, I don't want to bug you... but I *really* need to call my parents. And I'm so sorry but they're actually overseas right now, in Europe, and I could hear what your dad said about Germany and I just... I just need to call them, please. Can I use your phone? Please..." Ashley's voice quivered, and if I hadn't sworn she was *el diablo* reincarnated, I would have been pretty sympathetic.

I tossed it to her without making eye contact.

She called her parents, letting out a little cry when they picked up.

We drove in awkward stillness while pretending we weren't all listening. Apparently, Ashley's parents were on an anniversary trip, and while they said they had watched the news, they thought it was an exaggeration. Yes, they had heard rumblings of similar stories coming from other parts of the country. Yes, people were leaving to catch flights back to their hometowns, but they said it was all propaganda and it was just another ploy to run Americans out of their country. They never asked how she was faring, but they did tell her that her brother Chet, a star quarterback at U of A, said not to worry. Not one question about the pageant, how she was getting home, or who she was with. What a couple of a-holes.

I now remembered that Ashley's bigshot brother was the shining star of the family. I don't even think her parents had ever been to one of her pageants. Even though Celia wasn't what you would call warm, she would have at least inquired about my well-being.

Ashley hung up, her face expressionless. She handed the phone back to me. This time she was the one who didn't make eye contact.

I cleared my throat. "Em, Porke—I mean, Parker, do you want the phone? I kinda' lost yours back in the hotel. Sorry about that..." I held my phone out in offering.

He shook his head. "It's fine. With all that chaos, I would have been more surprised if you still had it. Actually," he said, looking uncomfortable, "I talked to my dad when you were passed out. After seeing what we saw in the hotel, all I could think was could be anything from zombies, to terror attacks, to well, again—zombies." He gave a small laugh and shrugged. "Nerds, am I right?" He glanced at his sister. "I don't know if you know this, but our dad's a top pharmaceutical scientist, at least in his field. He said some pretty freaky things about how he might know what this whole thing was. The governor's office made him and his colleagues lock themselves in at the CDC—Center for Disease Control—because they're basically the only guys in the States who might be able to figure out how to stop what's going on. I guess they're trying to figure out for sure what this is before more people get hurt." He patted his sister's hand as she began to cry. "He was trying to get us tickets to come home before his phone went out."

Bernice blinked her puffy eyes and looked ahead. She must be missing her dad like crazy. I remembered that their mom had passed away a few years back, which meant their dad was probably their whole world. I let out a sigh as I realized that this now applied to me as well.

"Sounds like you're in a hurry more than I thought!" Cookie made a sharp right before speeding up. "You need to eat somethin' first or you'll fade away. Hell, all y'all are spread out like a cold supper!" She made another sharp turn and rolled to a stop. "Welcome home!"

Cookie had pulled up to a house that looked to be the size of the Mercedes-Benz Stadium. She caught my look in the rear view and belly-laughed. "Lawd, you ain't even seen the inside yet! Growin' up I was so poor I had a pet tumbleweed. But I worked my ass off and now Cookie is the owner of strip malls all over the US and Canada. That's why Monique is the flyest one on the stage. No offense, sugar," she said, winking at Ashley.

"That's the second time you've mentioned this Monique," said Porker, unbuckling his seatbelt.

His door opened, and the ninja stood on the other side. The figure bowed while Porker stared, his mouth agape.

Cookie's loud laugh was contagious and the ninja bent over, giggling while we stood around like doofuses. The ninja stopped laughing and pulled his bandana down.

Whoa. Okay, plot twist. *She* pulled *her* bandana down.

"Wait, you look familiar." I narrowed my eyes.

"That's mighty kind of you, Ms. Abbott," beamed the pretty young girl in front of me. "You're kinda' like my pageant hero, I've been following you forever."

"Ah, Monique! Yes, now I remember! You're in Division 11 through 13. You're like, really good!" My smile was wide and I felt the first bit of happiness since the day had started. It was nice to have validation, and she even said I was her favorite! In front of good ol' Ashley no less.

"Kat is definitely one of the best, Monique," said Ashley, looking angelic while leaning in to give me a nudge. Like we were pals. Just because we were lucky sperm club members didn't mean we were chums. *Ugh.* She really had a way to ruin things. She obviously was trying to get a dig in by saying "one of the best" instead of "THE best."

"Can we *please* go inside?" Bernholdt tapped his foot impatiently. He rocked his injured arm dramatically.

Lucy sighed and Robert oafishly clapped her on the back. She grimaced and moved closer to the house.

"Okay, inside, inside!" Cookie ushered us through the large front door. Our mouths dropped at the opulence. She wasn't lying when she said the interior was bananas. She must have been richer than the guy who invented the Internet. The twins, Ashley and I all lived pretty close to each other in an upper-middle-class suburb and attended the same school. But compared to Cookie's place, we lived in squalor. In the middle of the hall, a large fountain with a naked lady spat water several feet high. Expensive-looking art decorated the walls—one even looked vaguely like a Warhol.

"Okay, Cookie's gonna cook up a feast to make your head spin. But in the meantime, Monique is going to show you to the bathrooms. The house generator was built to last through World Wars Three *and* Four. You'll have enough hot water to make you feel human again. Monique, grab some clothes for Ms. Ashley and Ms. Bernice." She looked me up and down. "Grab something for Ms. Katherine while you're at it."

Monique showed us each to our room with our own shower. As I stepped inside the steamy bliss, I shuddered in rhapsody. I turned the shower dial until it was hotter than a jalapeño's coochie and scrubbed the day away from my skin.

Getting out, I slathered myself in expensive-smelling lotion and allowed myself to look in the mirror. Utter relief overwhelmed my body as I saw that I looked like the me I was familiar with. Which meant I looked bangin'. Fox-hair eyelash extensions made my big eyes appear huge, and my spray tan was holding strong.

I strolled into the bedroom, feeling cocky, feeling normal. But my face fell when I saw what Monique had put out for me. The leggings weren't bad, but the t-shirt...well. It sure was special. I grabbed the tank I had been wearing and sniffed before jerking back. How my beautiful body could produce such a foul smell was boggling. I warily put the clean shirt over my head, bracing myself for comments as I walked out of the room and toward the smell of cooking.

Porker bit his cheek, trying not to laugh when he saw what I was wearing. Lucy was more obvious and burst out in howling laughter. Even Robert gave a small smile.

For some reason, Monique had decided that my new look would consist of a tee at least three times too big that read

"PLEASE TELL YOUR BOOBS TO STOP STARING AT MY EYES."

I held my head high and walked to the kitchen island like I was in my pageant gown.

"Monique, you scoundrel! You found my t-shirt drawer!" Cookie looked delighted.

It was time to change the subject.

"I gotta' ask…" Porker said, drumming his fingers on the kitchen island. "What's up with the ninja gear? I mean, I'm completely grateful for you saving us and all. You just, what, had it readily available as a just-in-case?"

Monique brightened. "It's part of my talent routine. I have an aerobic act where I do back flips to Bon Jovi and throw firecrackers every time there's heavy bass."

"The judges go crazy for it!" said Cookie, sticking her head out of the refrigerator. "She pulls for a Supreme title every time she yanks that one out."

I was impressed but hid it. In just a few years, Monique and I might both be competing for Miss Universe. She was young, but she didn't need any more encouragement to get to my level.

"Goodness, it smells delicious!" Ashley lazily walked in and stretched. Her taut stomach was a reminder that whatever Cookie was serving I would only eat half. She caught sight of my tee and her irritatingly symmetrical face brightened.

"Twins!" She pointed to her chest, which Porker and Robert gladly took as permission to look. Pervs. They hadn't even looked *once* at my lady parts when I walked in.

Ashley too had on a graphic tee which, by the look on Cookie's face, she found as hilarious as mine.

"I GOT CRABS AT JOE'S CRAB SHACK," shouted the thin fabric covering Ashley's tatas.

Wow. If pageant royalty like Ashley and me got such shitty tees, I couldn't even imagine what Bernice would show up in.

"Well, well, don't you look adorable!" Cookie stopped putting out plates of deliciousness (all carbs, unfortunately for me and my childbearing hips) and gave a whistle.

Bernice turned red, but for once, she wasn't doing her annoying crying thing. Probably because Monique was a traitor and had given her a plain white tee instead of the monstrosities she'd bestowed upon Ashley and me.

"Okay, kids, time to eat!"

Porker and Bernice beelined it for the table and started heaping their plates with mountains of sweet rolls, collards, cheesy grits and what looked like chicken fried steak. Everyone else followed suit and began tearing apart the food like they were reenacting Oliver Twist. I stared in visible disgust and sighed loudly. Everyone ignored me and continued to chow down like savages. I couldn't remember the last time I ate in front of people. My normal diet consisted of green juices and protein smoothies. In fact, I could totally relate to kids in Africa, as I too was literally starving all the time. Not eating in public made my lack of school friends that much easier, because I usually spent lunch in an empty classroom watching old pageant routines on my phone. I sighed even louder while taking extremely small portions of Cookie's spread. Celia would have been proud at my restraint. A sharp twinge hit my stomach and I forced her out of my head. Now wasn't the time to think such thoughts. To justify my portion control, I allowed myself a spoonful of the grits. Cheese and my digestive tract got along like a Cowboys fan at an Eagles game, but a couple of nibbles would be just fine.

The first bite, as small as it was, punched my taste buds high into my head. I moaned like a porno star and coughed to cover it up. I hadn't eaten in hours, and Cookie was too good a chef to deny my stomach this heavenly sustenance. I just didn't want anyone to know about it. I slowly ate my food while the others went back for more. They chattered and laughed while I sat alone, pretending I was deep in thought and not wishing someone would pay me some damn attention. Obviously, the spray tan wasn't going to be the conversation starter I was hoping for, but I knew what to say to bring back the focus.

"I sure do hate to be a party pooper, but my daddy said flights are still leaving from the local airport. It would be a shame for us to miss a chance to go home today because we're too busy eating." I made a point to look directly at Ashley.

Bernice looked torn between getting a third mountain of food or going home. Porker pushed his plate away and stood up.

"Ma'am, I do hate to eat and run, but Kat here is right."

He turned to Monique, who was still dressed in her ninja duds. "And you, missy, well...I don't think I'll ever be able to say enough to express my gratitude for saving us."

Monique flushed at his compliment. Well, if there wasn't a first for everything. A female who actually blushed at something that came out of Porker's mouth.

"Yes, thank you for all of this," said Bernholdt, cradling his arm. He didn't look so good. He was sweating through his button up and his eyes looked bloodshot like he'd been drinking stale moonshine. "I'd like to go with you to the airport if you don't mind."

Robert decided that he and Lucy would join us as well. Then Cookie made all of us take leftovers for "something to snack on," and we were off.

"Cookie, you didn't lock your front door. What if someone breaks in?" Parker asked, buckling his seat belt.

"Honey, if someone needs something, then I'm not going to stop them. My granddaughter and this car are the things I care about most in this world. It's those two I'll protect until I get carried out in a casket.

Logically, that didn't make sense, but I didn't come from a home big on charity. Celia once made a Girl Scout cry, just because the young'un asked if we wanted to buy Thin Mints.

The rest of us buckled up and I gave one more look at the house before turning back at our generous hostess. Cookie put the car in reverse as we backed out of the driveway. I should have felt ecstatic that I was on my way back to Atlanta. Instead, I had a bad feeling deep in my gut, and for once, it wasn't because I had eaten dairy.

CHAPTER 6

The eerie silence that had oh-so-bothered me earlier was now gone. Cars and RVs jammed the highway, all heading to a promise of safety. Sirens blasted from all directions, seemingly stuck in the same molasses-like traffic. Helicopters littered the sky like angry bees. My daddy hadn't said much about any happenings in Georgia, but I knew from experience that just because nothing is said out loud, it don't mean squat.

Lucy was glued to her phone. She wouldn't shut up with updates, no matter how far-fetched they seemed. Everything from Asia being unreachable to one site claiming that the Queen of England had been detained after eating one of her guards.

"Oh no! TMZ says that Justin Bieber's face was like, chewed off by a fan at one of his meet and greets!"

"Apparently, something good *has* come out of all of this," muttered Bernholdt.

Lucy ignored him and went back to scrounging for gossip.

"I *so* don't miss having my phone. It's actually kinda' nice to not be around that constant technology, you know?" Ashley said to me, leaning in like we were close friends.

Only Ashley could make me go from calm to insanely irritated in less than five seconds. Next, she would say she also never watched TV and that she only listened to NPR podcasts. God, she was so phony. It still boggled me that no one else was rolling their eyes every time she opened her mouth.

Choosing to ignore her, I closed my eyes, feigning sleep. I couldn't wait to be back home. I was going to crash for an entire week and then I was going to do everything in my power to switch schools and pageant circles so I would never have to see Porker, Bernice or Ashley ever again.

"Cookie? Would you mind dropping off Lucy and me back at the hotel? If you can get through?" Robert asked from the back.

"Sugar, are you sure? It didn't look like the safest place for you or your young one." Cookie looked skeptical.

"I couldn't stand it if we didn't look for Basil. We'll be fine. I have your number if we need to bug you again. Can't thank you enough for picking us up the first time." Robert patted Lucy on the leg as she continued to ignore him, jabbing at her phone's screen more aggressively than ever.

The SUV took a sharp turn, and we rode for a few minutes until we came upon the hotel, which was now completely engulfed in fire.

"I can't drop you here. Not in good conscience. Please reconsider," Cookie pleaded.

"We have to do this." Robert unbuckled his seat belt. "It looks calmer out here than it did before. I've played enough Call of Duty to finagle my way around. Besides, Lucy here will be a good lookout, won't you, sport?"

"What*ever,*" sighed Lucy. She opened the door and shut it, Robert scrambling close behind.

Cookie hesitated, watching the two as they waved, then walked off.

"Good riddance. Fewer people means less hassle." Bernholdt sniffed. "Now let's go. I can't imagine it's smart of us to loiter around here much longer."

The SUV rolled off, with Cookie giving one more look behind her, and soon, Robert and Lucy were nothing more than leftover sadness and anger.

I had won plenty of titles in Beaumont (Little Miss Swamp Monster when I was eight was a prime example) but had never been to the city's airport, as Celia was terrified of flying and would only pick pageants within a reasonable driving distance. Seeing the long line of cars trying to get to airport parking made my anxiety flare. How were we supposed to bypass all these folks if they were trying to get out just as badly as we were?

A loud rapping noise made Cookie roll her precious Caddy to a stop. She rolled down her window. I clutched my arms to my side, prepared to jump out of the car if any of the buffoons I was riding with said anything that would mess up my chance at that week in bed.

"Well, hello, sugar." Cookie smiled, seemingly unfazed.

"Ma'am, that's Private Bentley to you." The young man drowning in his fatigues tried to look stern, failing miserably. "Please pull up ahead. Someone will assist you before you're allowed inside." His voice was steady, yet his finger shook as he pointed to where we needed to be.

Cookie nodded and we drove silently to our designated spot. She put the car in park and hesitated before turning off the engine.

"Y'all sure you don't want to wait a day or two? Until this gets under control some?" Cookie's eyes met mine in the rearview mirror. They were shiny with something I hadn't seen since meeting her—fear.

"We have to get back," I said, speaking quickly before someone else could say something stupid. "But thank you. We'll be just fine."

I grabbed my small bag of the items I had snagged earlier and paused before opening the door. Celia would have whopped me if I didn't at least say a thank you to the people who had been unbelievably kind and brave to take us in. I opened my mouth.

"Thank you *sooo* much, Cookie," said Ashley, in that breathy voice of hers. "You are an angel. An absolute angel! And Monique, I will never be able to pay you back for saving us. Remind me to never do a pageant that you're going to be in because that ninja routine would beat my baton twirling any day."

Porker and Bernice also gave their thanks, and even Bernholdt managed a few graceful words. Since Ashley had pretty much said *exactly* what I was going to say, I could feel myself turning an uncomfortable shade of red as everyone stared at me. Monique smiled encouragingly.

"Eh... yeah, ditto." I shrugged like I didn't notice Cookie's sad face and Porker's disappointed expression.

Damn Porker decided to be a suck up and continued to talk to Cookie while I tapped my shoe impatiently. People were shoving past us to line up while soldiers yelled unintelligible orders through bullhorns.

"Ouch, watch it!" I stumbled back and turned to the offender, fists clenched.

"Sorry about that, miss, I wasn't watching where I was going." A tall, come-to-life Ken doll stared at me, blinding me with a face that proved there was a God.

I crossed my arms, trying to hide as much of the embarrassing t-shirt as I could. I discreetly got into my pageant pose—stomach pulled in, chest out, eyes twinkling brighter than that diamond the old lady from *Titanic* dropped into the ocean.

Okay, spray tan. Time to work your magic.

"No worries. I'm not made of glass." I laughed, as if I was a carefree gal who hadn't just spent my last few hours dodging monsters.

My confidence soared as I saw him check me out, smiling the whole time. Who would've thought—me meeting my future husband on the worst day of my life. I didn't have much experience in dating, as Celia had always threatened she would take a shotgun to any male I brought home that wasn't part of the Bush family. Plus, tap on Tuesdays, singing lessons Wednesdays, gym sessions with my trainer, and updating my social media to show everyone how great my life was didn't leave me much time to have a lot of friends, let alone a boyfriend. But I did know male judges, and I knew what made them sit a little straighter in their chairs with a slightly guilty look when they realized I was but seventeen.

"I'm Private Williams, but you can call me Remi. And you are…"

"Going home. She's not from here." Porker appeared by my side, stepping in close.

Oh, my Lord. Two men trying to get my attention like male dogs after a bitch in heat. I knew the proper thing would be to act embarrassed, but honestly, after Ashley getting some of my limelight I couldn't help but feel the sides of my mouth twitch upwards. If I had had time to Vaseline my teeth who knew what would be happening. Maybe a real fist fight would take place! It wasn't right to ask for more bloodshed, but after my last few hours, who could blame me for wanting a little TLC?

I bit my lip and gazed at Remi through my eyelashes. I totally ignored Porker, which wasn't an easy feat with someone of his girth.

"Well, I was *trying* to get home so I could, er, help the Red Cross. With, uh, with helping the less fortunate." I shrugged toward the airport's chaotic, growing line of panicked folk. "I've always been someone who cared more about others than myself." I gave a soft smile like the one I imagined Mother Teresa gave to those with leprosy.

Zac Efron's double paused and gave a glance to the front entrance.

"I'm not supposed to do this but let me check if I can get you guys ahead and inside. There isn't a lot of room left. They're being really strict about who they're letting fly out. Wait here and I'll see what I can do." He gave me his great smile and turned to go to the front, allowing me to check out firm glutes and a broad back. Wow, our grandkids would get a kick knowing how Grandma once checked out Grandpa!

Porker cleared his throat. "Well, I hope you don't feel the need to prostitute yourself to get us in. I'm sure we can figure out another way without compromising your virtue."

I was in too good of a mood to bite back. I mentally gave him the bird before waving to gather everyone around. Porker harrumphed, miffed about something no one cared about, least of all not little ol' *moi*.

"Okay, we're safe and we're heading home!" I had to yell to make sure the group could hear me. Cookie's car was still lingering outside and I wanted her to also hear we were going to be fine. "My new friend Ken, er, I mean, Private Williams, is going to get us inside." As if he heard me, he beckoned to me from across the line. "All right, follow me!"

Like a smokin' hot female Moses, I led the way through the sea of people that needed a bit of forcible parting.

"Watch it, lady!"

"Hey, no cutting!"

"Get in back like the rest of us!"

I ignored everyone, even though Ashley, Porker, and Bernice apologized to everyone yelling at us. Bernholdt was quiet, probably because he agreed with me. He was obviously smart by the way he spoke so, no duh, he was on my side.

We reached the front without any bruises, just lots of dirty looks.

"I got you all in. Head toward the stairs and you'll find food and cots. Get your flight set up as soon as you can so you can get out of here." He leaned in. "They're still trying to figure out how all this happened, but right now they want to get healthy people to the safe zones. Just to make sure, no one with you has been bitten, right? The army just issued some sort of warning that they think the sickness is spread by bites. A few cases have been from infected fluids going into open cuts and stuff, but mostly, it's all been by bites from those who already have it."

I looked at Bernholdt, who looked worse than if I had drawn him with my left hand. Well, this was a situation. On one hand, Bernholdt *had* been bitten. On the other, he might be my only ally, and I needed people on my side. Besides, he had only been nipped by a child, who was most likely just pissed there wasn't candy on the flight. Bernholdt was probably totally fine.

"Nope, all bite free here!" I flashed my pearly whites, hoping it would distract him enough from seeing the way Bernholdt was cradling his arm.

I ignored the pang of guilt and followed my beau through the door, ushering the others along. I promised myself I would keep an eye on Bernholdt, and if anything were to happen—which it wouldn't—I would figure something out.

People rushed past us frantically from all directions like Midwest women during a Kohl's sale. It looked like we weren't the only ones who had experienced whatever the hell was going on outside. No one would be in this much of a rush if they hadn't.

"Please tell me you already have flights set up." Remi kept his eyes on me, ignoring everyone else, and more importantly, ignoring Ashley.

"Yes! I do! I have a ticket being held. I'm all ready to head out." I quickly gave thanks to my dad.

"What do we do if we don't have tickets?" Bernice's quiet voice wavered as she looked at her brother, panicked.

"Oh. Well, I haven't met anyone inside who didn't have tickets. I mean, I guess you could try. I think Super Budget Air and Bus might have seats."

Bernholdt groaned. He was starting to smell so bad he could gag a sewer rat. I wished I had some Febreze to spray on him. I couldn't believe no one had noticed, and I needed to make sure it stayed that way. I wasn't going to get kicked out of here just for being a good person.

"You guys will figure it out. Who cares how long it takes to get home, as long as you get there, right?" I gave Bernice an awkward pat on the back, keeping up with my image of a caring young woman. In reality, I couldn't give two shits about these hangers-on. If they had to hitch home, then so be it. It wasn't my fault I had a prepared parent.

"Well, I'll be getting my ticket. I'll make sure to see if there are any extra, and, if so, I'll make sure I get those saved for y'all."

I had no problem lying. Hell, I lied at almost every pageant I had won. For Miss Arabian Nights, my stepmother insisted on my application that I was one-sixteenth Persian. Most kids' first traumatic memory was learning Santa Claus didn't exist. For me, it was catching Celia trying to forge my birth certificate to make me a year younger. I was only four at the time.

Remi led me to my airline's desk while the group glared daggers into my back. I don't know why they were complaining. *I* was the one who got us into a safe place. Geez, you'd think they could act a little more grateful.

"Hi, Meg, my new friend here needs to collect her ticket. Will you help her out? I need to head back outside, but I'll be back as soon as I can." He gave that smile and my knees went weak.

I turned around. "Hi, Meg!" My generous grin staled as I saw the way she was looking at me. She obviously had a thing for the private and that made me public enemy number one. We gave each other the fake enthusiasm of meeting one another as only girls can do.

"Hello. Can I get your confirmation number? I just *love* your shirt by the way. *So* cute. You can really pull off the homeless look!"

I understood her game, and ordinarily I would give it right back. But I was in a rush, and frankly, at this point of the day, I didn't give a damn.

I gave her everything my father had provided, and she punched some numbers into the computer. She frowned.

"I can see your ticket, it's paid for and there's a flight in a couple hours. But some weird message keeps popping up, blocking me from printing it out." She looked up and glared. "Are you on the no-fly list? You should have told me if you were."

It took everything inside me to not cause a ruckus. What a moron. I opened my mouth to ask for a manager.

Remi appeared by my side, huffing and puffing. "Hold up, there. All flights are canceled. At least for today and maybe tomorrow too. We just heard the CDC thinks Beaumont, of all places, could be ground zero. The majority of cases so far track back to this airport."

That tingling feeling I had after seeing Celia eat Todd's face as if he was made of pepperoni pizza came back until I felt as though cold cement was replacing my blood. "What... what does that mean?"

"I'm so sorry. It means you and your friends can't leave this building until we get our next orders. Also, the generator is low and we might lose power soon. That could lead to unhappy people taking out their frustration the wrong way and, frankly, we don't have the manpower to handle something like that. I have to go, but I'll try and see you when I get news. Hang tight. It'll all be okay. It has to be." Remi tipped his hat, his handsome face lined with worry. He tried to smile, and failed miserably, before running off.

I didn't bother saying bye to Meg the Horrible. I looked for Porker's red hair and ran his way.

I quickly told them what Remi had said, expecting them to give me the "you deserve this" look. No one did. In fact, they looked sorry for me, and Ashley's face held such sorrow you would think she actually cared about me.

"We'll figure this out. There's always a Plan B, we just need to figure out what that is. Let's grab some cots and food and make ourselves at home. And Kat, if we can borrow your phone, I know Bernice and I want to call our dad. You'll probably want to call yours again, right?"

I got my phone out. The battery life was almost gone, and I had left my charger in Cookie's car. I hesitated. I could easily say that it was dead and then secretly call my dad in the bathroom. But I was tired, and right now I didn't want to be the bad cop. I handed my phone over.

Bernice and Parker were quick and passed the phone back my way. My phone died just as my dad started to cry. I knew I should find a charger, but at the moment I only wanted to lie down, even if it was on a cot better suited for someone without my delicate bone structure.

We found an area and sat down, all of us wearily glancing around. Families around us comforted their children and elders. Celia had been a hardass, but what I wouldn't give to have her here, telling me my batwings needed toning. She had a sharp tongue, but I always told myself it was her way of saying she loved me. Before I could start feeling sorry for myself, I lay down and let Mr. Sandman work his magic.

I woke to darkness and random snoring. Someone belched like they were in the comfort of their home and not surrounded by a jillion strangers. It was probably Bernice. Or most likely, Ashley. I had seen the way she downed Cookie's calorie-laden buffet.

I rubbed my eyes until I felt more alert, then squinted as I tried to adjust to a room darker than a politician's heart. When I looked up, I saw an angular silhouette looming over my cot.

"Bernholdt?" I whispered.

The skinny man took a step forward, and moonlight lit his face. Red eyes peered into mine, and his salt-and-pepper hair was now white as snow. His nose twitched, and he slowly licked the back of his hand.

"Oh, God, not again!" I had half hoped it would be Remi standing over my bed, not an old man who was obviously so obsessed with me that even in this murderous state he was stalking me.

To my left, I saw Porker shoot out of bed as he karate chopped the dark air. He didn't have as much time to let his eyes adjust as I had, so he didn't see as Bernholdt crouched to all fours before leaping his way.

He smashed into Porker, who let out a yip as he fell back onto the bed. Others were beginning to wake. Bernice let out a shriek when she saw what was happening. She flew to her brother's side, trying to pull Bernholdt off.

Screams echoed around us. It looked like Bernholdt was just the start of our worries. A stewardess missing half her scalp scampered past us. Her blouse was drenched in wet red, but she still looked ravenous. Her eyes locked on an elderly woman who was trying to get away in a wheelchair. I looked in horror as the flight attendant ran her way before diving into the grandma, clamping onto her throat. The wheelchair tipped back and, as it did, a stream of blood shot through the air. I had watched enough *CSI* to know that kind of spurt only came from a severed artery.

Just a few feet above us, a white-haired freak swung from a handicapped bathroom sign. It was popping something that looked like baby carrots in its mouth. One fell at my feet, and I bent to pick it up before throwing it back down. Those were no vegetable snacks. They were fingers. The thing was eating human frickin fingers.

I turned from the horror and felt myself on the verge of gagging. I could no longer see Porker through the crowd of panicked people and even though we weren't BFFs, I hoped he was holding his own. I needed to get away from this sea of bedlam before one of *them* latched on to me. Just in time, I saw Remi running through the crowd, his wide shoulders hard to miss. Yes! Remi would get me out of here and back to Atlanta.

I waved frantically until he turned his head my way. Relief flooded my body as he charged in my direction. I kept my eyes on him and kept waving until I realized he was running just a bit too fast. I lowered my hand and slowly backed up. As he came closer, I saw that his left arm was gone below the elbow, and his nose, his beautiful nose, was swinging from his face like a tetherball. His eyes were still locked on mine as he sped up even more.

I couldn't believe that my future husband was going to be the one to end it all for me.

Looked like Celia had been right. I should have waited for a Jeb Jr. or a George. A dang Bush woulda' never tried to eat me.

"This way!" Someone screamed not far from me. "Everyone, the exit's over here!" Behind me, a door swung open and a swarm of bodies ran toward it, myself included. I leapt over those unfortunate enough to trip over abandoned suitcases and loose purse straps, trying not to look at the luggage carousel, which was slowly parading half-eaten victims around like lost baggage.

I peeked back to see a perfectly clear view of Porker, Bernice and Ashley fighting off monsters left and right.

Head back, Kat. It isn't too late to help.

Why? It isn't like they'd do that for you. Wasn't Celia always saying it's up to you to look out for YOU?

I ignored the stone in my stomach and kept my head down. And as I fought my way out the exit, I didn't look back.

Chapter 7

Outside, sirens blasted from all areas of the airport, muffling whatever the men in camouflage were screaming into their bullhorns. It was still night, but the Hummers and tanks had gargantuan sweeping spotlights, which made the shadows even bigger and the random echoes ten times scarier.

Feeling like I was back in the pageant room, I felt my skin bruise as flailing arms violently pushed and shoved me. I blinked, and the panicked crowd morphed from terror-struck families to kids with hair-sprayed bouffants and heavily made-up faces. A mere few feet from me, a bald man who looked like a clichéd substitute teacher slammed his elbow into a young woman (wearing a *horrible* shade of yellow) carrying a baby. She grabbed her nose and dropped the child. My eyes widened as she pushed Baldy away and dove after the fallen kid. As her head disappeared, a soldier who had obviously just "turned" (I was noticing the signs now—red eyes, streaks of white in the hair, and of course, the biggest clue—eating people) lunged into the crowd toward the woman. Well, I guess that took care of having to tell her that mustard wasn't her color.

The door I used for my escape flung open and a surge of petrified screamers poured onto the sidewalk. The ones in the back were too slow, and I saw a few creatures with white hair jump into the mob, pulling their next meals to the ground. Smells from the airport mixed with odors from the surge of people trying to make it out—blood, sweat and, if I wasn't mistaken, Panda Express.

I needed to get out of the way before I got caught in the Conga line feeding frenzy. Pulling my arms to my chest, I made myself as small as possible and scooted over to a wall. I looked at my options. There was no way I could go back inside. Even if it wasn't crawling with those "things," I couldn't stand the thought of having to run into Porker and the others. I didn't exactly ditch them, but I hadn't needed much convincing to get myself to potential safety.

Keeping my breathing measured, I looked for another possibility. The tightness in my chest eased when I saw Cookie's huge SUV still at the curb. I sprinted to it and knocked furiously on the passenger window while trying to keep an eye on what was happening behind me. I ran around the car, yanking on each handle, but they were all locked.

Damn it!

I kept knocking on the windows in case Monique had earbuds in. Cupping my hands around my eyes, I peered inside, and through the heavily tinted windows saw that no one was there. Only a lone pair of nunchucks lay abandoned on a floor mat. Stepping back in defeat, I caught a glimpse of my face and my colorless lips. I hadn't looked this disheveled since my make-out session with Digby McAlister after last year's spring dance—the one school social event I was allowed to attend. I glanced around, and when I was satisfied there was nothing with teeth coming my way, took a tube of lip gloss out. I might as well take advantage of the dark window's reflection.

Of course, I was in a hurry to find somewhere safe, but it could never hurt to look my best doing it. After all, as Celia used to say, there were no ugly women—only lazy ones.

It felt delicious to feel a touch of normalcy, though the sound of grenades going off in the distance was a tad annoying. I leaned in to get a closer look. It was amazing what a little color could do for one's self-esteem. I pursed my lips and fluffed my hair. If I had to find a silver lining in all this, it was how thin I was going to be. No food and all this cardio were making my cheekbones more defined than that one time I got sick from the water in Mexico.

As I was admiring how good I still looked, a small blur in the tinted passenger window distracted my preening. Annoyed, I spun around, expecting an apologetic Cookie for not waiting in the car.

Bernholdt, or what was left of him, stood on one leg in front of me. The top of his lip was torn, giving him a permanent snarl. His red eyes stared at my neck, unblinking, and the theme song from *Halloween* strummed in my head.

Shit.

My beauty had always been a blessing and a curse, and here was the utmost proof. Bernholdt, even in his disarrayed gory state, wouldn't leave me alone. Blood leaked from his effed-up mouth onto his cardigan, and I was surprised that I found myself hoping the plasma wasn't Porker's.

Bernholdt's stomach grumbled. His tongue darted in and out of his mouth, kinda' like mine used to after pageant season was done and I was in the drive-thru lane at Chik-fil-A. He crouched into a position I was beginning to know all too well and sprang toward me.

Choking back a scream, I stuck my arm out to hold him back. He strained against me, his teeth chomping frantically to get a taste of my Georgia meat. Long lines of drool flung against Cookie's car. He shook with excitement, his nose twitching with every bite he tried to make.

My free hand searched for anything useful in my pockets. A lipstick fell out, along with several small eyeshadow pods. If the goal was to turn Bernholdt into a contestant for *RuPaul's Drag Race,* I would have been just peachy. Bernholdt moved closer, his head shaking angrily, his eyes narrowing.

I refused to be eaten by a man who wore black socks with brown loafers. My fingers pushed deeper into my back pocket, and I let out an ecstatic squeal as they brushed against something metal.

I pulled my hand out and with the strength of Arnold Schwarzenegger in his early bodybuilding days, sank a L'Oréal nail file deep into Bernholdt's chest.

Bernholdt howled and lunged backward, swatting at the file. My moment of relief from having him off me faded as I realized he was still alive. How was that possible? I had held my hand to my heart during the National Anthem enough times to know I hadn't missed. He should be on the ground, either dead or very close to it.

Bernholdt stopped swatting and swung my way. Crud, why wouldn't this damned Yankee just leave me the hell alone?

I had nothing left to fight him with, just my desire to survive. I held my fists up, ready to give it my all.

Bernholdt took one hop my way, into the street, just as a truck painted like a Confederate flag sped into him. Bernholdt flew into the air before smashing into a Hilton hotel shuttle.

A Toby Keith ballad about how America was number one wailed from the truck's speakers. The door opened, and a man with about as many teeth as a twenty-year-old cat had lives leered at me, motioning for me to get in.

I was pretty certain if I got in that truck, ol' Billy Bob here would think I owed him something; the hell if I was going to lose my virginity for a chance to find out if men with big trucks really *were* lacking in the downstairs department.

I wrung my hands as I looked for another escape route, but other than sacrificing myself to the demented crowd that covered the sidewalks, I came up with nothing.

The redneck was getting agitated and unbuckled his seatbelt. He hopped out and adjusted the crotch of his jeans. He hawked a loogie, missing my foot by an inch.

"Now, lookie here, hun, don't be such a fuss bucket. Just 'cause you got you a nice pair of titties don't mean you gotta' be so stuck-u—"

A wrinkled, liver-spotted hand shot out from under the truck and locked onto the redneck's ankle, forcing him to fall forward. He screeched as he hit the ground.

I ran to him and stooped down to see what was grabbing him. A geriatric, white-haired man was attempting to bite his flannel-clad prey while pulling him to the curb. An oxygen mask was strapped tightly to his nose and mouth, keeping him from getting his dinner on.

"What are you staring at, you dumb bitch? Grab my arm!" A vein in the redneck's forehead pulsed. His oil-stained hand reached out, ready to grab onto mine.

Celia had been meaner than a toothless rattler at times, especially if I messed up during a routine, but she would have *never* called me such a foul word.

Crossing my arms over my Dolly Partons, I glared at the redneck as he called me every name under the sun. He began to claw at the cement, wailing pathetically as the old guy dragged him away.

I crept to my feet and climbed into the truck, giving a quick prayer in thanks to Jesus for dying for my sins. I was *really* racking them up today.

Toby sang for me to "drive it on home," and I cranked the gear into place.

I pressed the gas pedal and slowly moved forward.

CHAPTER 8

The truck sputtered sluggishly as I eased my way through the lane. Smoke obscured my view, blocking all directional signs, not that it mattered. Obviously, I should head home right away, but with my phone dead, that meant my map app wasn't available—and since I wasn't a hundred years old—I could read an actual map about the same as I could read Latin. Not at all.

I glanced in the rear-view mirror and like a sign that the powers-that-be weren't all that bad, I saw a small group of survivors walking awkwardly toward Cookie's car, dodging stray explosions and white-haired freaks. I mentally clapped in elation as I spotted Porker's red hair and made a U-turn. I knew they would be just fine. Now they would probably spend the next few hours waiting for me, but I was about to make them real happy when they saw I was just a mere few feet behind them.

Chuckling, I put my hand against the wheel to give a honk. But before I could see if it would play a Dukes of Hazzard tune, the SUV sped off.

What. The. Fuck!

Those belly-grazing bastards! Not even half an hour had passed since we were separated and they were already leaving. I bet they didn't bother to search for me. I mean, yeah, I probably should have stayed and stuff, but if any of them had the chance to get away, I bet they would have taken it just like I had. Those jerks had probably faked that they were in danger, just so I would be separated from the group. I bet right now they were laughing about my possible demise, all while heading to Cookie's house where they would stuff their Judas faces full of sweet potato pie.

My insides turned hot. No one left Katherine Abbott, much less losers like Porker and Bernice. If my phone was working I would have *so* posted a selfie with a passive-aggressive hashtag—something like #ThankTheBigManUpstairsForRea lFriendsNotFakeOnes or #TooBlessedToBeBurdened.

I needed proof that they were thrilled to have left me behind. Cookie's car pulled ahead and I followed. Thanks to *Law & Order* daytime reruns, I knew to keep my distance. Luckily, with all of the dead-ish people crowding the roads and cars full of people trying to escape, it was pretty easy.

We finally got to Cookie's house, just as the sun was rising. She pulled up to her mansion while I parked a couple of houses down. This damned truck stood out like a brown floater in a public pool—and I hoped the distraction of the world apocalypse would be enough to keep me hidden.

Sure enough, when they climbed out of the Cadillac, they gave zero indication that they could see me or the hideously designed truck.

I expected them to be joking and high-fiving when they stepped outside. Instead, they looked incredibly somber. Ashley and Bernice held each close as they shuffled inside.

I waited until the door closed before sneaking up to the house, peeking inside the nearest window. Bernice was pacing the floor, her face red and angry-like.

"I don't care what you say. Kat ran away. She doesn't give two potato spuds about any of us. She's so stuck-up she thinks the sun comes up just for her."

"Now hold on just a minute! You don't know what was going on in her mind!" Ashley winced as she attempted to stand. "If you hadn't found me under all that luggage you all mighta' thought the same thing about me! It isn't fair to blame Kat. In fact, we should probably go back and try to find her. Poor thing is all alone!"

A vein started to throb in my neck. Ashley was only saying that to look like she was pure and good. I had practically invented the "nice game." I knew Ashley couldn't care less if I was alive or dead.

"I'm with Ashley. Who knows what really happened. There was a lot going on, and it was dark." Porker stopped talking and chewed on his thumb.

Hearing Bernice speak so poorly of me stung, and my cheeks warmed. I always had a suspicion that Bernice stayed in pageants because she thought of me as her idol. I mean, she sucked, and she lost time after time (to me, almost always), but she continued to do them.

I backed away from the window, still crouching. I had imagined I'd storm into the house, accusing them of this and that and getting my rocks off at seeing how ashamed they would look. There was no way I was going in and apologizing like a wuss, so that meant I had to wait and listen some more so I could find out when they would stop being so pissy.

I was concentrating so hard I didn't see the fast-moving shape until it ran into me like a juiced-up linebacker. Smashing into the ground, I saw clouds turn into stars as my breath got knocked out of me. I gasped for air, struggling to get away from what once must have been a polished housewife—who was now snapping at my neck like a rabid cougar. Grabbing a fistful of hair, I shoved her face into the ground as her body convulsed against mine. Still holding onto her head, I karate-chopped her in the throat (Taekwondo being my talent at Miss Athletic Wear & Tear) hoping to stun her into slowing the eff down. It just seemed to make her angrier, which made her faster than a drunk during last call. She latched a manicured hand onto my ankle, her red eyes blazing as she crawled up my legs.

I let out a scream and tried to back away, but the extra weight from her obviously plastic tatas pinned me beneath her. My chest fought to catch air, but the fall, plus her body mass, made it difficult. All I could do was watch as she moved her way to my head, her nose trembling in titillation as she stared at my forehead. A red stream moved past my eye, and I realized I must have cut myself when I fell. I screamed again, hoping Porker or someone would hear. She stuck her tongue out to lick the blood coming off and I flung my head from left to right to stop her.

My one free hand searched the ground for a weapon. I hesitated as I wondered what good it would do. These things obviously didn't die easily. Hell, I lost my best nail file in a man's heart and it didn't do squat. I cleared my head of negative thoughts and strained my hand further.

The housewife howled as I smashed the first thing my hand found, a decent-sized rock, against her temple. She leaned away enough for me to scoot backward. My eyes roamed for possibilities. I could either try and make it to the door or fight this bitch until one of us met our maker. I saw a pair of shears lying on the lawn where they had been abandoned and ran to them.

Another howl made me spin around just as my predator lunged. I held my weapon in front of me and closed my eyes.

A heavy thud—then silence—met my ears. I slowly opened one eye, then the other.

The shears had gone through the woman's left eye socket, piercing the back of her skull. She lay completely still. Brain matter covered my hands, and my adrenaline surge suddenly left me. I let go and stepped aside as the housewife crumpled to the ground. The force of her falling pushed the shears to go even further into her head, and the top of her scalp slowly opened into several sections, much like a Blooming Onion at Outback Steakhouse.

"Holy hot cakes, you killed one!"

Porker's joy pulled me back into the moment. I allowed myself a quick breath before turning around. I wiped body fluids and clam-chowder-like chunks onto my pants and stood defiant, waiting for the crew to rip me a new one.

"Jesus! You couldn't have come out five minutes earlier?" I growled.

"Sorry, we only just heard the commotion. I swear I didn't know you were in danger." Porker looked sheepish enough for me to believe him.

I didn't have time to respond before Bernice flew at me, giving me a huge hug. Cookie and Monique looked delighted to see me, and Ashley was beaming. Porker was staring in amazement at the really-dead-this-time thing, before walking over and prodding its body with his foot. It still didn't move.

"Sugar! My grandmother always told me the *rougarou* were impossible to kill. You proved us wrong!" Cookie nodded in approval.

"What's a… a rougarou?" I asked.

"It's what us in Louisiana call a creature that doesn't die. Like a werewolf."

"Do you know how many of those things we tried to kill? Hell, I saw one guy shoot one in the chest a million times and it still kept walking. Do you know what this MEANS?" Porker was getting excited and he bent down to examine the woman's head. "It means the only way to kill them is brain penetration. Which means we finally know what we're dealing with. Not vampires, not creatures from the black lagoon. Not even, sorry Cookie, a rougarou. Folks, what we have here are most similar to zombies."

I laughed. "Zombies? Seriously? You're joking, right? No way. Besides, I thought zombies only ate brains."

Porker shook his head impatiently. "No, no. These things are totally zombies. The whole crouching, nose twitching thing threw me off. But these things are obviously dead and then come back to life. Well, life-ish. Plus, they eat flesh, and the infection spreads through bites, at least that we know for sure. The final proof is how they're killed—by destroying the brain."

"Okay, say I believe what you're saying. That doesn't explain how my stepmom got sick. She was never bit—and I'll tell you what, if Celia had been bit, the whole frickin hotel would have known about it."

Porker was quiet. "Hmm, good point. I think it's time to call my dad again. I have his office line, something I'm only supposed to use in emergencies. I think this would count." He looked at Cookie, who was clutching Monique to her side. "It's also time to get home. Let's get in and figure this out."

Everyone headed back inside. I stopped Porker before he could get inside.

"There's no way you didn't hear me earlier. It was *way* too loud. Why didn't you come out?"

Porker was quiet, then looked me straight in the eye. "You left us at the airport. Now we're even."

He followed the others in, leaving me in total shock at the doorstep.

CHAPTER 9

I didn't meet Porker's eyes as we crowded around Cookie's phone to call his dad. I was miffed, of course, but oddly enough, I was *proud* of the ginger. I understood revenge; I just didn't know he had it in him. There was just no way in hell I would tell him that, and I planned on ignoring him so he'd know not to cross me like that ever again.

Porker plugged in a phone number and turned on the speaker. The phone was picked up before the first ring finished.

"Hello?" The voice on the other end sounded exhausted and scared, two things you never expect to hear from a real adult.

"Dad, it's me, well us. Bernice and me."

"Oh, Parker, oh thank God! We got news that the Beaumont airport had been compromised and when I didn't hear from you right away I thought…" His voice trailed off. He coughed off what sounded like a throaty sob. "Where are you?"

"We're still in Beaumont, at a new friend's house. I'm with two other people from Atlanta, actually from school and that pageant stuff." Porker ignored the way the females in the room stared at him.

"Good. That's good you're with others—strength in numbers." Yelling in the background covered up what else Porker's dad was mumbling.

"Dad, I can't hear you that great. What's happening over there? Do you have any idea what this is? We just found out the infected can be killed if their brain is destroyed. Actually, one of the girls I'm with now was the first to make an actual kill." I felt him look at me, but I kept my eyes on the phone. He was probably giving me praise to get me one step closer to forgiving him but I wasn't going to let him atone so easily. I kept my face as emotionless as possible.

"You've been that close to one of those things?" Porker's dad sounded horrified. "You need to stay away from them, at all costs! And do not, I repeat, do NOT get bitten by one." His voice became a whisper. "We know what these are and we know what the virus is, but we don't know how the hell it got out of the CDC."

"What... what do you mean, Daddy?" Bernice leaned over the phone, her usual band of sweat pooling at her hairline.

I heard the sound of muffled footsteps and a door closing. "The department was working on a controlled virus at the lab—N1T3. It started as an experiment to test life extension for soldiers. Something we could inject that would make a soldier stronger, able to take hits in battle and still live. This version also enhanced basic motor functions—the need to eat and survive. In doing that, it depleted the need to sleep and to feel emotion. It was aimed at creating the perfect soldier. One who sought and destroyed any enemy that wasn't carrying the same virus they were. My team was tasked to find an antidote. Something that could undo the effects so a soldier could take the N1T3, then take a reversal and resume life as a private civilian. The mice we infected did exactly what the virus was meant to do. But soon, after just hours, sometimes minutes, they began attacking our techs as they tried removing them from their cages, and the less we fed the mice, the more crazed they became.

"Then... then Dr. Shen Ming was bitten. Just a nip, nothing we all hadn't seen before. But per protocol, we placed him in isolation. Less than two hours later, his hair turned white, his eyes became red and he was throwing himself at the glass, teeth bared, with what looked like the same psychotic mannerisms as the infected mice. We tried to feed him food, but all he paid attention to was the meat. He would tear at it like a... like a rabid animal. We threw a lab rabbit in with him and he had torn it in half with his hands and jaw before it had time to hit the floor. We attempted to give him our newest version of the antidote, but to no avail." The twin's dad was harder to hear as the noise in the background grew louder and more chaotic. He was breathing heavily, his words becoming clumsy. "What we know, without a doubt, is that one hundred percent of the bites will turn a person into some sort of cannibalistic super-human. Blood coagulates quicker, allowing faster recovery. It's aided by protein, something the host will recognize it needs, such as human flesh. We don't know how this got out of the lab, but it did. Terrorism is high on the list. Either way, it isn't good." Porker's dad suddenly stopped speaking. Loud knocking and more yelling filled the background. "The strangest thing is that we're finding out Beaumont might be the source. With all of the planes coming in and out of the area, it's easy to see how this spread so quickly. We just can't figure out how or why it's happening there."

Bernice had turned the color of a vintage wedding dress, and she began to sway. I moved away in case she was going to throw up. I wouldn't have blamed her; the words coming out of her dad's mouth were scarier than Celia's had been during her "lady time."

"I have to go." Porker's dad began speaking quickly, his voice going in and out with static. "I'm trying to send a helicopter to pick you all up, but the only contact I've gotten ahold of is at Arnold Air Force Base in Tennessee. I need you and whoever you're with to get there. Can you do that?"

Porker's face was full of panic. He looked at me, and I nodded like I knew what I was talking about. I would have said yes if Porker's dad had asked us to drive to Utah to become confirmed Mormons, as long as it meant I was one step closer to getting home.

"Yeah, Dad, sure. But why can't we just drive straight to Atlanta? Going to Tennessee will take us a few hours extra, won't it?"

A sad sigh came across the line. "When's the last time you've heard what's happened in Atlanta? Or any main city?"

Our silence gave him his answer.

"All major roads are closed, either by military or, most likely, abandoned cars. You can't get in or out unless you use back roads, but we're hearing even those are being run over by those... those things. When you drive to the base, you'll have to be careful. Very, very careful. You know now not to take a highway for longer than you need to. There're a few routes you can take that will get you to Tennessee without being blocked. Just keep a lookout for the infected. They're fast, which it sounds like you already know."

Cookie leaned in over the phone. "Mister, my name is Cookie. I know these back roads you're talkin' about—no problem there."

"Good... good... My kids... my kids are my everything and I don't know what I would do..." The static grew stronger and his voice became louder. "Get there as soon as you can and ask for Colonel George Martinez. He's only there for a few more days but he said he'll take care of you. And whatever you do—don't drink the water!"

There was the sound of a struggle and panicked voices. I barely made out someone yelling that Dr. Ming had broken through the isolation glass before the phone went quiet. Porker tried to call his dad back, but it went straight to voicemail.

"Now I've heard it all." Cookie fanned herself before plopping down on the nearest seat. "I always knew the government was crazy, but this—this is on a *whole* other level."

"I need to call my dad!" I grabbed the phone from Porker and dialed a number I knew by heart. The phone rang three times before the line went silent. I pulled the phone back and saw it still had power, but it was now reading "No Service." I forgot about being mad at Porker and shoved the phone at him, my hand trembling. "Fix it! You called your dad, and I need to call mine. Why is the phone saying it doesn't have service?"

"Oh, honey, I was afraid this might happen." Cookie heaved herself out of the chair and came over to look at her phone. "Fear is an awful thing, and it makes folks forget about responsibilities and such. This is a time to be with family. My best guess is people are leaving their jobs, including those who control these cell phone tower thingamabobs, to get home and find some safety. I don't know technicalities, but I do know human nature."

I threw my arms up. "Great. Just great. So, what you're saying is we're screwed. I mean, without a phone, how can we get to Tennessee, let alone back to Atlanta? I don't know how to read a map. Do you?" I looked pointedly at Porker who shook his head.

Cookie looked at Monique who was clutching the arms of the chair she was sitting in.

"I'll take you there. Monique and I will take you."

"That's mighty sweet of you, but you don't even know us. And you've already done so much for us." Ashley said out loud what I too was thinking.

Cookie sighed. "When I took in Monique after my daughter passed, I knew I would make every decision for her well-being. This is for her as much as it is for you. If Parker and Bernice's daddy think they'll be safe at this military base, then maybe they'll take us in too. I know how this works. Services and power get shut down and people panic. They'll loot stores at first, then they'll hit the rich neighborhoods, like this one. If we can get ahead of that mess, then me driving y'all will be worth it."

"I don't know…" Porker turned to his sister, but Bernice was still ashen as hell and looked to be on the verge of crying. What a shock.

"Well, then allow me to speak for the group," I chimed in, "when I say we'll gladly accept your offer. Us humans need to stick together, and Cookie, I'm not going to lie when I say your map-reading skills will be mighty helpful. I *literally* don't think I could even get from the kitchen to outside without my phone." I stood wide, a move I once read online was looked at as a power move. Porker's mouth opened and I made my stance even larger. This wasn't a time for Southern manners. This was the one chance we had available for us to get home, and, apparently, as I was the only one who had a lick of sense, then I would be the one to make the decision.

Porker's mouth was still open when the lights began to flicker before shutting off completely. The house grew quiet as all appliances stopped their humming.

Just as quickly, they turned back on.

"Shit." Cookie stood straight, her eyes wild as she looked around the room. "Shit!"

"What's the matter? Uh... isn't it a *good* thing the power came back on? And like, this *fast*?" Bernice stared at Cookie, her cow eyes blinking slowly.

"Baby girl, ain't you never seen news footage from Katrina? If the power is going out around here, then this house is going to stick out like a sore thumb being all lit up and such." She paused, staring off into space. "Okay, three things. First, we need to shut this generator off. Second, we need to grab supplies. Parker, you grab water, *bottled* water, and any type of food that will last without needing refrigeration. Monique and I will get blankets and pillows and such. Bernice and Ashley, you two are in charge of anything around the house you think we can barter with. I have some painkillers for my sciatica in a kitchen drawer. That would be a good place to start. And Katherine, honey, you're in charge of clothes."

"Roger that." I started to move, then stopped. "Wait, what's the third thing?"

"Weapons." Cookie's face hardened. "And I know just where to find 'em."

CHAPTER 10

We scattered to our stations. Normally, having to pick out clothes would be a process I would enjoy immensely, but everything Cookie owned was larger than a size 12. That might be perfect for Porker and Bernice, but as someone who had been introduced to micro-greens before Hollywood made it a "thing," I knew nothing here would fit me. Or, if I wanted to be honest, Ashley. However, I didn't want to keep wearing this ridiculous tee, and as much as I wasn't Ashley's number one fan, I couldn't let her go around wearing her "I Have Crabs" tee, either. And *no,* it wasn't because she made the shirt look kinda' cute in a hipster kind of way.

I grabbed some bags from Cookie's closet and began to throw in pieces that we could—gag—recycle within our group if need be. Sweats, hoodies, tees *without* embarrassing phrases and, just because I damn well felt like it, I stuffed a handful of cocktail dresses from what looked to be from Cookie's pre-carb cooking days into the bags. I noticed a couple of shirts that weren't hideously huge hiding toward the back and eagerly snatched them off their hanger. I tore off the shirt I was currently wearing and slid a deep-purple silk blouse with eyelet and lace detail over my head. It was a little loose, but it felt like Coco Chanel was giving me butterfly kisses as the fabric slid sensually across my skin. This shirt would have totally cinched me a win at the Miss Future New York Model, which I was supposed to be in next week. A bubble rose in my throat as I realized my pageant life wasn't going back to normal anytime in the near future. Unless they came up with something like "Miss Undead" or "Miss Don't Shoot Me I'm a Human!" pageant, I was officially retired. Considering I had participated in and won the supreme title at a pageant called Little Miss Ranch Dressing when I wasn't but eight years old, anything was possible.

I fell into a deep squat and flung the bags over my shoulders and back before slowly standing straight. I gave the closet one more glance to make sure I hadn't missed anything.

Heading downstairs, the sound of doors banging and footsteps running across hardwood floors echoed off the high ceilings. I nudged the bags off me and wiped my sweaty lip. The lights were off again and the heat from outside was creeping in. I sniffed under my arm and jerked my head back. I hoped to hell someone had the sense to grab deodorant because what I was smelling could bring tears to a glass eye.

"Okay everyone, time to pack up the car!" Cookie bellowed. Porker was behind her, huffing and puffing as he struggled to carry plastic bags full of kitchen goods. Ashley and Bernice were close behind, each carrying an armful of random stuff. Monique was standing next to Cookie, and as she moved forward, I saw that her neck and shoulders were heavy with sashes, and she was carrying as many crowns as her skinny arms could hold. She saw me looking and her ears turned pink before slowly moving her arm to reveal a make-up belt. I smiled wide and gave her a wink.

We stuffed the car with our finds, then waited for Cookie to speak.

"Sugar, you know how I've told you stealing is bad? And to never EVER do it?" Cookie looked hard at Monique.

Monique nodded slowly.

"Well..." Cookie exhaled, scratching her wrist. "Sometimes, there's... exceptions. And I never want you thinkin' what I say next is okay. But we need help, and who we're going to take from is a bad, bad man."

Monique's eyes lit up. "Is it Buck?"

Cookie chortled, then tried to look serious. "Yes, sugar, it's him."

"Who's this Buck?" Bernice had finally stopped looking so ashen. Her voice only quivered slightly, which was an improvement from earlier.

"He's a racist S.O.B. who lives next door. Monique and I moved here to this neighborhood a couple years past. We'd just unloaded the U-Haul when this pot-bellied man comes into the yard, shootin' a pistol into the air, scaring Monique half to death. He claimed he was aiming at a tree rodent, but I've seen that look before. It was the same look the five-and-dime owner used to give me when my cousins and I would come in for ice cream, years ago in Baton Rouge."

"He's a surv... a survivor?" Monique looked quizzingly at Cookie.

"It's 'survivalist,' sweetheart. One of those loonies who thinks the world is out to get 'em and stores guns like a squirrel hoarding nuts. He's gotta' have enough weapons to fight off anything that tries to come between us and Tennessee. I also know he's in Florida, probably at some white trash convention. Which means his house is empty. Except for all those rifles…" Cookie looked at Porker, then me, turning her back to Monique. She lowered her voice. "We need to get to them before anyone else does. You four have the luxury of heading home. Monique and I still have to fend for ourselves. I haven't asked anything of you yet, but this… this I need help with. Please."

"Yes, of *course*, we're going with you. You don't need to ask us twice. Just tell us what to do and we're in." Porker surprised me again with his strength. I didn't know where it was coming from. Maybe Doritos cheese dust gave him some sort of special power. Whatever it was, I was glad he was taking the lead.

"Well, alrighty. Let's do this." Ashley flipped forward and tied her long hair into a waterfall of a ponytail. She glided gloss over her lips and put a hand on her hip. For a moment, she looked so much like a blonde me I felt myself mimic the hip move.

"Okay, here we go." Cookie looked at Monique. "Honey, you need to stay in the car. Just in case. Just lock up the Caddy until you see us."

Monique held her head high, whispering, "Yes, Nana." She didn't cry, but for the first time since I met her she looked her young age.

Cookie started out the door and we followed close behind. The sun was shining like it was a normal day, its rays equally bathing Cookie's mansion and the almost-beheaded housewife, lying in a pool of dark blood at the front of the house.

A yellow sports car sped past, the first car I'd seen in Cookie's neighborhood besides her precious Caddy.

"Are you NUTS? You need to get outta here!" the driver screamed, shaking his fist.

He sped past without stopping. A suitcase tied clumsily to the top of his car flew off, but he didn't slow down.

"Alrighty then. Time to get in the car," said Cookie with forced brightness, opening the Cadillac's door. She snapped her fingers, and Monique pulled her gaze away from the fading Porsche. She looked teeny as she climbed into the monstrous SUV. Cookie motioned for her to lock the doors and looked at the rest of us. She had an unsteady smile on her face that didn't do much to hide the fear or distract from a pool of sweat collecting at her décolleté.

"Here we go. Everyone, stick close together. It's just next door, but it's a big-ass house, and I don't know exactly where he keeps what we're needing."

Cookie moved down the street and we hurried to keep up. She walked up to the door and after a moment's hesitation looked back at us.

"Damn! I didn't think about not having a key..." Cookie stared at the massively tacky lion-head door knocker.

Ashley bent down and picked up a rock.

"Cookie, it's fine, looks like Ashley found one of those hidden key rocks." I waited for Ashley to turn it over.

Instead, Ashley brought her arm back then flung it hard. The rock flew through the living room window with a satisfying smash.

"Welp, that works too." Bernice took off her sweatshirt and wrapped it around her fist. She and Ashley walked up to the broken window and Bernice broke off the rest of the glass.

I was the first one to close my mouth. Glancing at Porker, he too was wide-eyed in shock as his sister shimmied her way through the broken pane.

Bernice opened the door from the inside and motioned for us to come on in.

"Well, hell, would ya' look at that?" Cookie stepped inside and walked toward a huge painting of a beer-bellied man in a camouflage suit. A woman in a blue sequined bikini was lying at his feet. Both of them were holding large guns, and the bimbo was holding it in a *very* sexual manner, making me glad Monique wasn't with us.

Cookie barked a short laugh. "Lordy. What's scarier? This or people eating people?" Cookie's hand skimmed the canvas, before using her pointed nail to cut a line down the middle of the man's crotch. She stepped back and smiled. "Better. Much better."

"Look!" Porker stepped by her, pointing. "Did you see that?"

Through the cut Cookie had just made, something metal shimmered. Porker grabbed a piece of the painting and pulled back. I joined him, then Cookie, as we tore the canvas apart completely.

"That didn't take long to find!" Ashley whistled as we took in a wall of guns, knives and other goodies.

"Woo hoo, load up! Grab anything and everything, and remember to grab bullets!" Cookie handed us all plastic bags she pulled from her pockets.

Even though I was born and raised a Southern belle, I had never been into guns or hunting. Plus, as a pageant girl, to have calluses would be worse than finding a stray chin hair. Celia had a small collection of guns, but she had a whole room in our house dedicated to her doll collection, of which she transferred her obsession to me. Looking at the wall of guns, I wish she had at least taught me how to pull a trigger.

I spotted a pearl-crusted pistol and reached for it at the same time as Ashley. Ashley pulled her hand back and gave me a smile.

"Go ahead, it's yours." Ashley went back to grabbing stuff off the wall, and I grabbed my pretty gun before she changed her mind. I mumbled my thanks and went to wait by the door, no longer in the spirit of being greedy.

When everyone was finished, they met me by the door and we headed to Cookie's car. Monique must have seen us coming, as she was soon outside, opening the trunk door and stuffing back pillows with her shoulders.

"Um, I have something for you. It's not a big deal or anything, just thought you might want something else to wear." I put my pistol inside, then pulled out the only other shirt I had found in Cookie's closet that was a smaller size. It was a black chiffon, bell-sleeved blouse that would have looked amazing on me.

"Oooooh, Kat, this is beautiful! Thank you so much!" Ashley held the shirt in her hands, beaming.

"I mean, it's whatever." I shrugged, not making eye contact.

"Hey, want me to clean that cut on your forehead? I have bandages and a small bottle of peroxide in one of my bags. That zombie housewife dinged you pretty good."

I touched my forehead and winced. God only knew if there were any plastic surgeons still alive, and I really didn't want a scar. I nodded and gave a small smile.

We piled into the SUV. The constant tightness in my chest faded as I watched everyone laughing, getting along like old pals. Plus, Ashley was being nice and not just the fake kind, the *real* kind that Celia said didn't exist.

Ashley sat beside me and brushed my hair off my forehead. She blew gently on my wound before placing a Band-Aid over my cut. She smiled, gave my arm a little squeeze, then leaned forward to make conversation with Monique.

I watched how they spoke and laughed and felt a tinge of envy at their ease with each other. I had never had a female friend outside of Celia, and I didn't know how to even begin to be a good girlfriend.

As I continued to watch the two girls, I realized maybe I was ready to try.

CHAPTER 11

Cookie, much like my daddy, kept US maps in the car, most likely as something to sop up fast-food coffee spills rather than for reference. One of them looked older than the culotte pants trend. Cookie had marked it with a red pen to show the back roads we needed to follow to get to the base, and for the hell of it, from the base to Atlanta. The marks looked like nothing more than squiggles, but I nodded seriously as she explained the route like I understood old-timey talk.

Monique turned on the radio, but all that met our ears was static or eerie silence. AM gave us one scratchy option, but it was mostly just a voice screaming Big Pharma was trying to get us to buy pills to drive up stocks and that the infected were just actors, that this was another American conspiracy trying to divide the country. Blah, blah, blah. Cookie sighed and leaned over, popping in a CD. Soft rock you usually hear in dentists' offices played gently, and Monique drew her legs to her chest as she gazed outside.

I, in the meantime, tried to keep my eyes anywhere but the outdoors. Already, I had seen several people run past, tears dribbling down their faces going who knew where. A small group that *must* have been from hippy-dippy California held signs reading "Zombies are People Too" and "Dead People

Deserve Rights." Maybe Celia was lucky not to be around to see this. She most likely would have been arrested for breaking those wussy signs over her knee before whacking them aside their heads.

"Hey, what did your dad mean when he said not to drink the water?" The inside of my mouth was raw from chewing on it for the last hour. I tasted blood, which reminded me of the red squirting out of the Asian business man's stomach. That vision stopped the cheek gnawing.

Porker tilted his head, taking some time before speaking.

"It's just a guess... but I think it's another way this virus can spread. We know now this zombie-thing can happen if someone gets bit. Which I thought was maybe just a saliva deal. But my dad *did* say something about infected fluids. So that could mean, ehhh, like... hehe... well..."

"He means pee and poop." Monique turned around and rolled her eyes.

Porker's cheeks flushed. "Yeah, exactly."

"So?" I raised my eyebrow.

"Well, when people die, their bowels usually, er, let go. So, if one of the first infected got into, say, the water tank, or a swimming pool at the hotel, that would explain how people got sick without getting bit. People showering and getting water in their mouths, unconsciously drinking chlorine water, you name it. As long as it was ingested, it was a way in. Maybe that's how your stepmom got sick, Kat. I mean, unless you can think of a time when she was bit, and I'm pretty sure you would remember something like that."

I racked my brain for when Celia first started to feel ill. We got to the hotel, we unpacked and ordered dinner (two garden salads, no dressing, no croutons) and my stepmother took a shower. I skipped it because I had been too tired to even brush my teeth while Celia took one of her famous forty-five-minute showers. The next day, with my stepmother not feeling great and me being in such a rush, I took a quick birdbath and chewed gum while getting ready. I was never in contact with the water, not like Celia.

My silence seemed to be an answer for Porker, and he had the courtesy to stop talking. We drove in silence, me replaying the night before the pageant in my head, trying to pinpoint exactly when Celia complained of not feeling right.

We crawled along the highway with countless other cars, and over two hours passed before anyone spoke.

"Babies, we need to get gas. The Caddy's near empty and we should buy some jerry cans to fill so we don't have to stop again. Imma' pull over at the next stop. I don't think I have to remind y'all to be aware of your surroundings."

The car slowed even more, then turned onto an exit with a gas station sign.

"Oh, Lordy be…" Cookie exhaled loudly and we all peered ahead.

A line longer than drunk girls waiting outside a club bathroom met our eyes, all for petrol, just like us. We drove to the back of it, waiting for our turn. I ignored the knot in my stomach as we crept along, feeling some relief when we were just a couple of spots behind the nearest pump.

A man came out of the convenience store and started walking our way. He waved his arms, motioning for us in line to put our windows down.

"Folks, I'm sorry but we're out of gas! Please move on. We're all tapped out!" The attendant moved down the line, yelling the same thing to each car. Angry honks and plenty of flipping off met the man's words.

"Oh, hell no!" Cookie looked back at us, her nostrils flaring. "We do NOT have time to wait in line for another hour. I don't think Caddy can take it, and I am NOT getting us stuck on the side of the road with those blood-suckers. I have a wad of cash that has to buy us at least a tank of gas. You kids wait here. I'll be right back."

"Cookie, wait!" Porker's hand shot out, pointing ahead to a man crouched down next to a convertible BMW. Looking closely, we could see him filling up a red gas can, one of ten all neatly lined up. A scrawny, second attendant stormed out of the office. He nervously tapped the guy on the shoulder. We couldn't hear the words, but before he finished yammering, the fuel nozzle crashed into his face. The startled employee stumbled back. Blood cascaded from his nose and mouth.

"Monster! It's one of those monsters!" A woman standing outside a mini-van screamed hysterically. She threw her kids inside, glancing back at the attendant, now bathed in gasoline and blood.

"He musta' just ate someone! He's covered in blood!" Someone else joined in and threw a bottle at the young man's head.

Screams and shouts filled the air as the panic grew from car to car. A church bus peeled out, the gas nozzle still attached. The pump ripped out, smashing into everyone who didn't dive out of the way. From our close vantage point, we could hear the sickening thuds as bodies smashed to the pavement and into the store window. A severed leg caught onto a windchime and spun bloodily with tinkling ceramic fishes.

Monique started to breathe heavily, her tiny hands clutching the sides of the seat. Cookie grabbed her and pressed the lock button.

Porker disappeared before I noticed he had even opened his door.

"No!" Bernice reached out for him and frantically unbuckled her seat belt as she made a move to go after him. Ashley held her arm out, stopping Bernice from leaving the SUV.

"Wait. Just wait. Parker's smart. He has to have a plan." Ashley held Bernice's hand, and Bernice slumped against her, burying her head in Ashley's shoulder.

I ignored them all and held my breath as I watched to see what Porker was up to. His quickness was still a surprise. He ran like a linebacker, not like the video-gaming, Slim Jim lover he looked to be. He gained speed as he reached the convertible owner. His hand balled into a fist, and he brought it forward, connecting with the man's throat. The man bent down, then fell to the ground, seemingly gasping for air. Porker grabbed four cans, stacking them awkwardly, before speed walking back to the Cadillac.

Bernice was the first one to react and started hollering words of encouragement as Porker dodged the terrified crowd like a real-life Whack-A-Mole.

Porker was so red when he reached us I couldn't tell where his skin ended and his hair began. He wheezed as he shoved the cans into the car.

"Cookie, open the gas tank!" I jumped out to help Porker and grabbed a can, opening the nozzle and began pouring the much needed fuel into the Caddy.

When it was empty I threw the can aside (littering being the least of my problems) and jumped into the car, Porker behind me.

Cookie started the SUV and we peeled out.

I watched everyone congratulate Porker, clapping him on the back. Ashley gave him a big kiss on the cheek. I copied their smiles and offered a convincing "Good job," but as Cookie and I locked eyes in the rearview mirror, we seemed to be the only ones who understood that this wasn't a victory.

It was just a momentary distraction from what could possibly be awaiting us ahead.

CHAPTER 12

Dusk was upon us before long. My stomach was grumbling, but it was nothing compared to Porker's. He looked mortified every time his stomach roared like a lion stepping on a Lego.

"We need to stop. We all need food and sleep, and I don't want us driving in the dark. That's just gonna make us a moving target to all sorts of baddies." Cookie saw I was about to speak and she hushed me with one look. "We'll leave first thing in the morning, and we'll get to the base in just a few hours—plenty of time for y'all to catch that helicopter home."

"That sounds good to me, Ms. Cookie." Ashley stretched her neck, trying not to wake Bernice, who was sleeping on her lap.

"Nana, there was that sign saying a motel was coming up. Can we stop there?" Monique rubbed her eyes and yawned loudly.

"Sugar, I don't think hotels or motels are a good idea. We should stay away from paying places. I just have a feeling, can't explain it, but my Spidey senses are telling me we should look for any other type of place... like a—"

I cut Cookie off. "Like a church?" I poked our driver slightly as a small, run-down building with a cross on the top came into our view.

"That'll work!" Cookie pulled into the dirt parking lot and drove toward the back before putting the car in park.

"Do you think we need any, um, backup?" Porker asked, motioning to the weapons in back.

"Good call. I also have a hatchet in the trunk. Looks like them church-goers boarded up the windows. We're gonna have to break them down to get in. Depending on who or what's inside, the hatchet could come in handy for other reasons." Cookie crossed herself and bowed her head. "Hoping it don't come to that."

We exited the SUV and headed back to the trunk. Porker grabbed the hatchet, I took my little pearl-handled gun (that I still didn't know how to use), and Monique held her nunchucks with determination. Ashley and Bernice grabbed various pistols, with Cookie slinging a shotgun over her shoulder. Cookie kept Monique close as we cautiously inched ahead.

The door was padlocked shut. Cookie told us to step back, before aiming the shotgun at the lock and firing. The lock split in two and fell to the ground. Porker opened the door slowly. Behind it was a wall of different-colored wood, all nailed shut from the inside. Porker raised the hatchet, swung it down in the middle of the wall, and split the wood easily. He kept hacking at it until there was enough room for us to squeeze through. He poked his head inside and turned back to us, shrugging.

"I don't see anything. It's still pretty light inside—doesn't look like they shuttered in the stained glass above—and I don't see any dust. I also don't see any of those *things*, so we should be good to go in."

Cookie disappeared as she walked inside, her shotgun at the ready. We waited, holding our breath, and not relaxing until she came back out.

"Parker's right. Let's grab our things and settle in for the night."

We carried in pillows and blankets, plus food and bottled water. Once inside, we shut the door, and Cookie began to spread out our bedding on the ground. She stopped and turned my way.

"Kat, will you and Parker look for food? We'll set up the beds."

"No problem." Porker and I moved to the back, where we discovered a little kitchen. I opened the fridge and found it was still slightly cool, even though the electricity was turned off.

"Jackpot!" I held up some cheese and fruit.

"Great job!" Porker beamed at me and motioned to the cupboards behind him. "Ah-ha! Look what I found." He opened a cabinet door and exposed a wall of red wine.

I was never a drinker because first, empty calories—gross—and second, I had never gone to a lot of parties. Celia had me too busy practicing routines or standing endlessly for fittings. But right now, vino sounded pretty amazing. Just one glass. I was only a few months from turning eighteen so I was practically an adult. I grabbed a bottle, glad it was a screw cap, because I had no idea how to take out a cork. Porker swiped some glasses, and we grinned at each other as we headed back to the others.

"Lord, you teenagers, I swear!" Cookie groaned when she saw us with the wine. "That's the blood of Christ, not for getting toasted!"

"Aw, come on, Cookie. We've had such a horrible couple of days. Just a nip." Porker smiled widely at the matriarch, swinging the bottle her way.

"Hm…" Cookie sniffed. "Okay, but I'll deny it if anyone asks. And don't go thinkin' this is going to happen more than

this one time! One more rule... Cookie gets the first glass—
and make it a big one!"

Porker opened the wine and we clinked our glasses
together as if we were at a normal dinner party. The first sip hit
my bloodstream fast, and I knew I needed to eat. I turned my
back to a statue of Jesus, who seemed to be judging me with
his perfect abs, as I tore into a chunk of cheddar.

"Isn't it kinda weird that no one's here? The food in the
fridge was still fresh and there isn't even dust on the glasses."
I sipped my wine and leaned back against a pillow.

"It is. But maybe they all went home to be with family. I
think for once, we all just got a break. Now, my glass is getting
a little empty. We have any wine left?"

Bernice tipped the bottle over. "All out!"

"There's like a hundred more bottles in the kitchen."
Porker lazily pointed his hand to the back.

"I'll grab it!" Ashley sprung up. "Bernice, come help?"

The girls headed to the kitchen. Cookie tucked Monique
into her sleeping bag and snuggled next to her. They both
started to snore. Looked like the wine had hit Cookie hard.
More for us then!

"So, should we grab some holy water or melt down some
silver to make bullets?" I pointed to a table of goblets.

"Are you serious? Kat, Holy water is for vampires, silver
bullets for werewolves. We're dealing with lab-created *zombies*,
not mythical crea—" He stopped when I started to laugh. "Oh,
you're joking. Okay, you got me. I know, I'm a total nerd."

"I'm just teasing, Parker. You might be a *tad* geeky, but
you're smart and you helped us get this far without dying.
So... thanks." My ears warmed and I kept my eyes on my
glass.

"Wow… you just called me by my real name. Like, on purpose."

The warmth moved from my ears to my cheeks. It was time to change the subject. I didn't like this funny feeling in my stomach, and all of a sudden, I was very aware that Parker had decently nice forearms. I cleared my throat.

"Yeah, well, that wasn't too cool of me. I am sorry. Really. Won't happen again." I sat back up, pulling my hair back behind my ears. "Tell me the first thing you're going to do when we get back home."

"Besides take a shower? Probably grab a burger, covered in as much cheese and bacon as I can get my hands on, washed down with a gallon of sweet tea. And hug my dad." He grew silent, then sighed. "I just want my dad to be okay. Bernice couldn't deal if anything happened to him. She was devastated when our mom died…" He stared at me, wide-eyed, and put his hand to his mouth. "Oh, shit, I'm so sorry. Your stepmom…"

The wine grew cold in my gut and I was instantly sober. "It's fine."

"Do you… do you want to talk about it? About her?" Parker kept his eyes on me.

"*Gawd.* Where do I even start?" I began to pick polish off my thumbnail, watching little pieces of pink flutter to the floor. "My mom left right after I was born and my dad married his partner's assistant, like, two months later. Celia never wanted kids, just a husband who could take care of her. But my dad wanted us to bond, so she put me in pageants before I could even walk. It just kinda' took off from there. I started winning right off the bat, and when I got old enough to realize how good I was, and how much attention I was getting, I went in full force. I mean yeah, my whole life I've dieted, worked out like a pro athlete, and I've been waxed once a week since I was twelve. Waxed *everywhere*. I don't even know what my real skin color is because I've been tanning for longer than any skin doctor would want to know about. But just like any sport, you have to work at it to be your best."

"I guess I don't get it. Pageants seem horrible, especially after hearing the stories my sister would tell."

I looked at him in surprise. "They aren't awful, not at all. Pageants are great! The networking is amazing and the opportunities are endless. It looks great on a college resume, and the higher the title, the more you can do with your platform. Maybe they aren't for some people, but I was born to do this. Without competing... I don't know who I am." I fiddled with a piece of hair. "It was Celia that took it to the extreme. She had no interest in me, other than having a living doll she could brag about. You should have seen my diary when I was younger. It was filled with all the mean things she said to me, like the one time I wanted an ice-cream cake for my sixth birthday, and instead I got a protein shake with a few candles taped around the glass. Or the time I got really sick, and Celia still made me do a pageant, and I puked everywhere on stage. Turned out I had salmonella poisoning." I felt the word-vomit rise and rushed my next sentence without thought. "When I saw my stepmom, you know, go the way she did, the first thing I felt was relief." I laughed harshly. "I'm the shittiest person in the world. You can say it." My chest began to tighten and a tear slid slowly down my cheek.

"Oh, Kat, I don't think you're a bad person. Not at all." Parker reached out and wiped my tear away. He gently cupped my chin and lifted it so we were looking into each other's eyes. "You're perfect. You've always been perfect." He slowly leaned closer, his eyes never losing mine.

My heart began beating wildly, and my throat started to close. I, too, leaned closer, and my hand covered his. I closed my eyes and parted my lips.

A loud fart startled us both backwards. Cookie let out a loud snore, and another toot that sounded like a deflating balloon animal.

Parker and I began to giggle, each of us trying to stay as quiet as possible.

"Oh man, I would love a nightcap. Where the hell is my sister with our wine?"

"I gotta' hit *el baño*. I'll go look for them." I smiled shyly at Parker. "I'll be right back."

Heading to the back, I hummed a little tune, making sure to slightly wiggle my behind in case Parker was watching. I decided to check out the kitchen first.

"Yoo hoo! Where have you guys been?" My smile dropped from my face when I walked through the doorway.

Bernice was on top of Ashley, vigorously eating her face while Ashley lay twitching beneath her.

I shrieked, before grabbing the empty bottle of wine on the counter. I brought it up and smashed it onto Bernice's back.

CHAPTER 13

"Ow! What's wrong with you?" Bernice rubbed her back, glaring at me.

Ashley stood up. "Babe, are you okay?"

"Babe?" I couldn't close my mouth. "Wait, what's going on?"

"ARGHHH!" Cookie flew into the kitchen, with Parker close behind. She held a piece of a broken pew, stabbing it wildly in front of her.

Bernice and Ashley held hands, both red and blotchy from doing what I still didn't understand.

"Well, hell, I thought you had *turned*, Bernice! What in tarnation was I supposed to think, with you munching on Ashley like that?"

"Geez, Kat, calm down. You just caught a moment you weren't supposed to see. At least not yet." Bernice looked at Ashley, who slowly nodded.

"We... Bernice and I... well... we've been, um, *dating* for about three months now."

"What?" I took a step back, wondering if zombies could lie and if this was all a ruse. "But Ashley... you're so... so..."

"What? So beautiful? So popular?" Bernice finished my sentence. My flushed face couldn't hide the embarrassment that basically confirmed that was exactly what I was thinking.

"My parents basically disowned me after I came out to them a few years back. I just stopped talking about it and kept doing pageants, hoping that my mom and dad would see that I was still, like, super feminine. But they didn't care." Ashley looked sad for a moment, then brought her head back up.

"And why do you think I've been doing pageants for so long?" Bernice added. "Because it's just *sooo* fun to stuff this body into taffeta every weekend? Or maybe it's because I like hearing people laugh when I get on stage?" Bernice looked pointedly at me.

"Sorry for walking in on you two. I didn't mean to. I was just looking to see where you were." I bit back the rest of what I wanted to say. But I had recently deemed myself a changed person, and when I set my mind to something, I always did it. Except for learning how to French braid my hair. That was still on my to-do list.

"We all need sleep." Cookie brought us back into reality. "The sun will be up in just a few, and since I'm guessing Starbucks no longer exists, you don't want to see Cookie when she doesn't have coffee and is tired as heck. So off we go to bed." She looked at Ashley and Bernice. "Now, I know I let you have a little wine. But you two are sleeping separately."

"Good call." Parker looked at Bernice, mouthing "We need to talk!"

"Don't think you're off the hook, mister!" Cookie wagged her finger at Parker. "I saw the way you and Ms. Katherine were making moon-eyes at each other. You two are definitely sleeping apart." She shuffled off, leaving us all mortified.

"Okay, well, night everyone." Parker headed out first, giving me a little smile as he passed by.

I felt that feeling in my stomach again like I did before pageant officials announced awards. A thousand butterflies fought for my attention as they fluttered against my insides. I could easily guess my cheeks hadn't gone back to their normal color by the way Bernice and Ashley were smirking.

I walked out, head high, and made a bed far from everyone. I snuggled into the blanket, trying to not focus on the wood floor digging into my hip. *Please God, please don't make me rip one in my sleep like Cookie did.* I closed my eyes.

I slept soundly, without any dreams, or at least without remembering any. I woke to a gentle shake and opened my eyes to see Monique breathing into my face, a prompt that we all needed to brush our teeth before heading out.

"Nana said you and Parker are in love. Is that true? Have you guys, you know, K-I-S-S-E-D?" Monique's big eyes sparkled, and while I didn't want to talk about it, I was glad that at least one of us was in a good mood.

"A lady never talks about two things, Monique. First, is her age. Second, is what she does when the sun goes down." I winked at her, and she covered her mouth, giggling. "Now help me up."

I beelined for the bathroom, brushing my teeth until I could no longer taste the stubborn grit that had plagued me since my first sip of church wine. A good reminder to not drink in the near future. I smiled, glad the red hadn't stained my Los Angeles-white veneers. Before heading out, I grabbed paper towels and scrubbed my face and armpits. After putting my hair into a high ponytail, my fingers reached into my little toiletry bag. I pulled out pink lipstick and rubbed a little on the apples of my cheeks to give them color before dabbing some on my lips. I then took my small container of Vaseline, my main weapon in pageants and life, and swiped some on my eyelashes. It wasn't mascara, but it would do.

I walked out of the bathroom and right into Parker.

"Oh! Hey, there. Sleep okay?" He smiled at me, and, for a moment, I forgot how to speak. The same guy I once dismissed like a vegan ignores a lamb gyro was now making my throat close in an emotional allergic reaction.

"Yup. Yup. Slept great, thanks for asking!" I smiled brightly and turned away, quickly making my way to the main area.

My breathing was heavy by the time I reached everyone, my brain racing. Why the hell was I being so weird? I was used to men wanting me. Like, *hot* guys. One time, at a required pageant meet-and-greet, a local senator who used to be a pro football player gave me his phone number before Celia chased him off with an umbrella. So why the hell was an overweight, red-headed guy, who definitely wasn't even *close* to six feet, making me feel like I was in the presence of a younger David Beckham?

"Morning, Katherine. Nutrition bar?" Cookie waved some colorfully packaged goods my way.

"Sure." Normally I would have asked how many calories were in it, but between worrying about monsters and, now, a certain member of the opposite sex, I couldn't care less about meeting my daily macros.

We cleaned up our bedding and packed the car. Ashley and Bernice were giggling, acting extremely touchy-feely. Now that they were out, they weren't hiding their feelings. I couldn't believe I hadn't seen they were together, them being closer than a pair of buttcheeks since we left the Beaumont hotel.

Or maybe... maybe Ashley was just putting on an act. To get ahead with the judges. Maybe it was going to be her new pageant platform! Hell, in this day and age, that sort of thing could get a girl extra points.

Looking at them holding hands and being lovey-dovey put that theory to rest. Ashley wasn't a good enough actress to pull something like that off. I knew this for a fact as I'd seen her try to act out Reese Witherspoon's part in *Legally Blonde 2* where Reese finds that her mentor is the bad guy. She actually won Grand Supreme in that pageant but, obviously, it was just because the judges felt bad for her.

Bernice tucked into Ashley's arm and I rolled my eyes, but—and I would never admit this out loud—I was a wee bit jealous of how comfortable they were with showing affection.

"All right, kids, in the car we go! We have a big day ahead, with y'all heading home and such." Cookie threw in the last pillow and opened the doors for us to get in.

Parker quickly slid in next to me, and my heart began to beat louder than a Broncos fan cheering at the 2016 Super Bowl. He didn't look my way, but our legs touched slightly, causing a roar of tingles to hit my secret parts. I clenched my stomach and held my breath, looking out the window as though the sight of trees was the most fascinating thing I'd seen since walking in on Bernice and Ashley.

The SUV had barely made it out of the parking lot before Monique spoke.

"Um, Nana? I *really* have to pee."

"Child, I asked you a million times if you had to go before we left! Can you hold it?"

"I don't think so. Can't you just pull over and I can go behind some bushes?"

Cookie looked ahead, then slowed the car down until we were by a small river. She looked back at the rest of us.

"We'll be right back. Y'all lock the doors."

With Cookie gone, and Ashley and Bernice acting like newlyweds, the tension between Parker and me was way too intense. One of us had to say something.

"About last night... sorry if I made you... I don't know... uncomfortable. I thought you were feeling something that you obviously aren't." Parker wiped his hands on his jeans, still not looking at me.

"It isn't that." I sighed. "Parker, I think I might be feeling something. I just need some time, okay? There's so much going on and I... I just need time."

"Fair enough." Parker smiled as we looked at each other.

A loud scream from outside stopped our conversation.

"Oh my God! What was that?" Bernice opened the door and we followed her toward the noise. Parker held his hatchet, and as we got closer I realized he was the only one with a weapon.

Cookie's head bobbed up crazily by the river, and we ran her way. She was on her knees, pawing desperately at the water's edge. Monique was going in and out of the water, screaming when her head popped out for air. It was obvious what she was yelling about. A bloated zombie had Monique by the ankle and wasn't letting go. She needed to get out of the water before she drowned, or worse, before the monster discovered it had a taste for pre-teen flesh.

CHAPTER 14

"Grab the end!" Parker dropped to his belly at the edge of the water, reaching out the hatchet's handle. He didn't seem to notice when the blade he was tightly gripping ate into his palm. Blood dripped from his hand, going into the water. At the first drop, the creature holding onto Monique released its grip, letting out a frantic wail. It dove after the disappearing red, licking the water like a thirsty pooch.

Monique took advantage of the situation and kicked out to swim our way. Her foot smashed into the zombie's head, which must have been waterlogged; its skull made a popping noise as its forehead slowly caved in. The force of the kick pushed the zombie backwards and it floated away with the current, its tongue still probing wildly.

Cookie was halfway in the water before she reached Monique. Parker followed suit, and they lifted her out before collapsing on dry land. Monique shivered hard, her teeth clacking as if she was wearing ill-fitted dentures. Cookie held her so tight I was afraid Monique had escaped death only be smothered by her grandmother's double D's.

"Oh Jesus, look!" Ashley said, backing away from the water, motioning we should do the same.

Another bloated zombie clawed its way downstream. Then another. And another. Now that I was paying attention, I could see some stuck in between the river's rocks and fallen trees.

"We need to get away! NOW! There must be a hundred of those things!" I backed away, then looked around in case there might be some freaks in the bushes around us.

"Kat's right, let's go." Parker made a move to leave, then turned back. "Monique, were you bit?"

Monique started to sniffle. "I don't think so, Parker. But maybe Nana should check."

Cookie did her best TSA impression and patted Monique down, checking her skin. When she was finished, she hugged Monique to her chest, giving us the negative answer.

A high-pitched squeal behind us made us look toward the river to see one of the monsters grabbing a tuft of grass, pulling itself out of the water. Or what was left of it. Long tendrils of pale pink innards followed the torso and what appeared to be just one shattered leg. I now knew how fast these suckers could be, even without a set of stems.

"You guys, we should *really* leave now." I didn't protest as Parker grabbed my hand. We ran for the SUV, piling in as fast as we could manage. Our combined panic made it seem like the car had less room than before, and I found myself sitting on Parker's lap. I hesitated, then lowered my head onto his shoulder, muffling my sigh. His sweat mingled with mine. Parker didn't speak until our heartbeats slowed and our breathing returned to normal.

"You okay?" Parker's voice was low.

"I'm fine. I shouldn't have freaked out like that. You'd think I'd be used to them by now." I stared at the back of Monique's head as she sat curled up next to her grandma. I had an awful thought in my head, and now that it was quiet, it wouldn't leave my brain.

I turned and kept my voice soft so only Parker could hear me.

"Monique was in that water with a lot of zombies. Zombies that, for the most part, looked pretty torn apart. Do you think the water—"

"Do I think the river was infected enough that if Monique drank any by accident she has the virus in her?" Parker spoke like he too had thought of this. "I hope as hell not. But we'll find out. We just need to keep our eyes on her."

My lids grew heavy and I nestled into Parker's warm, fluffy chest that felt just like my Tempur-Pedic pillow back home. Between last night's wine and this morning's craziness, I was beyond pooped. I needed to close my eyes for a few minutes. Just to get some energy…

The gravel road lulled me straight into dreamland. I peered down to see I was wearing a scarlet princess-style ballgown, and my waist looked extra teeny. I smiled as I smoothed the fabric down, then stopped as I smelled biscuits growing fat in the oven. Looking around, it seemed I was back home, in the kitchen. Church music blared and Celia, who had her back to me, was fiercely whisking something on the stove.

"Oh, Mama Celia, I didn't see you there! Whatcha' making?"

She didn't answer, but continued to stir to the beat of *Great is Thy Faithfulness*.

I took a step closer and my stomach gave a greedy jump when I realized my stepmother was cooking her famous BBQ sauce to put on the pile of ribs that lay waiting beside her. My arm reached out for a rib, Celia ignoring me. I took a big bite and swallowed.

"Yum! Tastes better than usual! What'd you do different?" I wiped my mouth with a bit of the red dress.

My stepmother finally stopped her wild stirring and turned to me. Her eyes were gouged out, her teeth broken. The worst was what was behind her worn apron. Her flayed chest revealed that all her organs and ribs were missing. My eyes went from her body to what was in my hand, which parts of were now in my stomach.

Oh God no!

Celia began to laugh hysterically as she reached for the plate, throwing ribs and sauce over my face and hair.

"Kat! Kat, wake up!"

I gasped, blinking as I touched my face, which was wet. Monique was holding a now empty bottle of water, its contents I took to be all over me.

"I'm so sorry, you wouldn't stop screaming!" Monique looked terrified. Everyone did.

"It's okay. Uh… sorry about that. I had an awful dream about my stepmom and barbeque—" I stopped speaking as my nose caught a familiar scent. "Wow, I hate to say it, but Lord that smells good. Where are we? Did we stop for lunch?"

"Oh, no, honey, no, that ain't good stuff that's making that smell." Cookie spoke slowly like she was afraid of scaring me.

The group continued to look at me. Monique scuttled back to under her grandma's arm.

I looked out the window to see large piles of trash on fire. Water was still in my eyes, and I tried to blink away some of it instead of wiping, to keep whatever makeup might still be clinging on.

As my vision cleared I saw the bags weren't bags, but bodies. Torn apart, limbs missing, some still twitching, bodies.

My stomach twisted as I realized that the charred smell of human flesh was what had been making me salivate.

I threw open the car door and threw up. I didn't have much in my stomach, and everything seemed to come up with the first heave.

It was too late before I realized my inside contents were spewing over a pair of very shiny black boots. I wiped my mouth, then slowly moved my head upward to a young man in camouflage, smirking at me like I was a naughty toddler who had eaten too much glue.

"Welcome to Arnold Air Force Base, miss. If you're finished here, I can direct y'all inside to meet Colonel Martinez. He's been waiting for you to arrive."

My face flooded with shame. If the monsters didn't kill me, then the embarrassment from this moment might just do the trick.

CHAPTER 15

A gate topped with barbed wire rolled open while soldiers with large guns strapped to their chests walked past, not paying attention to us but rather what was behind the entrance. Shots rang out, causing me to jump. I looked back to see a handful of creatures twitching on the ground, fresh bullet wounds ripped through their heads and torsos. Two men in camouflage laughed and high-fived each other as they holstered their weapons. The soldier who had my DNA on his shoes seemed unaffected by the noise as he pointed to where we needed to park.

We got out of the SUV, and the horror of the past days fell into second place as I realized we had made it, frickin *finally*. Parker, Bernice, Ashley, and I would all be home by the end of the day, and in a helicopter no less. The twins and I would get to go home to our dads, while Ashley... well, her parents sucked, and hopefully they'd been eaten in a very painful way by Eurotrash zombies. It was a little sad that I probably would never see Cookie or Monique again, but I would have been more upset if I had to spend one more day in a city other than my beloved Atlanta, home of the Braves, and more importantly, home of at least 200-plus beauty shops that had enough shampoo to wash all this grime out of my tattered locks.

"Well, alrighty. I know what you ate for dinner, but I don't know your name. Who might you be?" The young soldier with the once-shiny shoes smiled at me, and for a second I forgot about my newfound feelings for Parker. Good Lord, this man was finer than Chinese silk. I had always had an appreciation for a man in uniform, as proven by my swimwear during Miss United States Army Military Loyalist. I wore a bedazzled thong one piece, and Celia had painted medals of honor on top of each tata. I knew I had won first place when Major Kurt Farris, honorary judge of the day, wiped a tear from his eye while keeping his other hand discreetly in front of his pressed khakis.

I flipped my ponytail and wet my lips quickly before smiling back. I stuck my hand out. "Katherine. Katherine Abbott."

"Well, Miss Katherine Abbott. I'm Private Harrison. *You* can call me Wes. I heard you all might be coming. They just didn't say the majority of y'all were models." He grinned at Cookie, who stood unmoved. "Let's get you something to drink while we wait for Colonel Martinez. He's a little tied up at the moment, but he told us to make sure you're all taken care of. Now, if you wouldn't mind following me, I'll get you fixed up." He smiled again, just at me this time, and for a moment, I felt like the old me.

"Wait, hold up. Where are the airmen?" Parker stopped, looking around.

"Good catch, my man." The private smiled. "We were called in to help man the base. Most of the planes were called out, which left the area vulnerable. We got here just in the nick of time. We heard of other bases who were overrun by the infected. Couldn't even get to the ammo." He shook his head, then smiled again. "Okay, back to it."

Private Harrison led us past a parking lot full of Hummers and a helicopter, to a large concrete building. Inside, we were escorted into a room with empty bunks that begged to be slept in. A large window faced the hallway.

"How's this, Miss Katherine?" Wes turned my way. "It's no Four Seasons, but at least y'all can rest up for a bit."

"Hm, I *guess* it will do." I couldn't help my wide smile until I caught a glimpse of Parker, who looked like I had sucker-punched him in the nether regions. My tummy panged with an odd feeling... something like... *guilt*? It couldn't be. I mean, it wasn't like Parker and I were "officially" together or anything. And I wasn't acting *that* flirty. And even if I was, I was doing it so Wes, er, I mean whatever his name was could see we were good guys. So basically, I was taking one for the team. Either way, I turned down my smile wattage. "Thank you, Private."

"Well, before I go, can I get you anything? Food?" Wes said the last part to Parker, who didn't acknowledge the dig. All of a sudden, the G.I. didn't seem as hot as he had a few minutes ago.

"We're fine, sugar. If you can grab this colonel then we'll be on our way." Cookie's voice was pleasant but held a bit of chill. I hadn't seen Cookie mad in our short time of knowing each other, but her tone made me think I'd rather walk into a gym shower without flip-flops than see her pissed off.

"Like I said, he's a bit... tied up. Y'all wait here and I'll see when he'll become available." He went to leave, then turned back, and I saw that his handsome gray eyes lacked warmth. He kept his smile as he looked me up and down, undressing me with his stare. I was used to men staring at me in a desirable fashion, but this… this was something else. I crossed my arms over my milk makers and scowled.

He left the room, followed by a clicking noise.

"Uh, did he lock the door?" Bernice walked over and jiggled the handle. She looked back at us. "Yeahhh, it's definitely locked."

Bernice walked back to us quickly. Behind her, out in the hall, the private was huddled with a small group of other men who kept glancing back at us like we were a zoo exhibit. One of the men gave a lewd look toward Ashley, and another at Monique, reminding me of the childless men who like to record teen pageants.

I began to realize this wasn't men acting like catcalling construction workers. Something wasn't right. Why hadn't the colonel met us as soon as we had arrived?

I looked at Parker to see what we should do. He took a deep breath and marched over to a large window facing the hallway. He knocked.

"C'mon guys, this isn't funny. Unlock the door, okay?"

The private walked to the window and faced us. "Shut up, fat ass. Jesus Christ, you're whinier than the girls." He sneered, his chiseled face turning uglier with every word he spat.

Parker's hand fell to his side. He turned, his skin spotty with embarrassment. He walked to us, and I saw shame flicker across his face. My breath began to quicken as my blood pulsed furiously through my veins.

Monique began to cry, distracting us for a moment. "Nana, I don't feel too good." She was glistening with sweat, her sweet face flushed. I made a step to go toward her, then stopped. Right above her left ear, a few lone strands of hair lay flat against her skin. The hairs were white.

I felt Parker's hand on my arm as he pulled me back to him. The hard grasp let me know that he too saw the white streak.

Cookie saw the way we stepped away from her granddaughter. She glanced down and her eyes widened. She quickly moved her hand to cover the white.

Monique continued to whimper as she clung to Cookie.

"Shhh, baby, it's gonna be fine. You're going to be fine." Cookie's throat quivered, though her voice held steady.

The door creaked open. "Now why the hell is she crying? I mean, *really*, we give you a nice place to stay and offer you something to eat and this is how you decide to act?" The private walked in, pointing a gun at us. Another soldier walked in beside him, also pointing his weapon in our direction.

Cookie stayed calm. "I'm sorry, mister, she's just scared. We think there's been a misunderstanding. Could you please get the colonel for us? Then we'll be on our way." She kept her hand on Monique's head to hide her hair.

Wes sighed loudly, tapping his gun to the side of his head. "I was hoping y'all would be different, or at least less dramatic than the other groups."

"Other groups?" Ashley spoke, her voice raspy.

"Oh, pumpkin, no need to be jealous. You're the best group so far. All that... fresh meat." He grinned, then licked his lips as his eyes roamed her body.

"Can you please find the colonel for us? Please? We want to leave now." Bernice's voice was barely louder than a whisper.

"Aw, sure, why not? Eric, open the door!"

Across the hall, a soldier threw open the door opposite from us.

Even through the thick window glass, I could almost hear the scream of the first man I locked eyes with, though his gag wouldn't have made that possible. Beside him, other men and women were stripped to their undergarments, most with tape around their eyes and mouths. Their heads rolled toward the opening door, all of them thrashing against their restraints. Eric shut the door.

"I hope you see what can happen if you misbehave." Wes exhaled loudly. "If you just *listen*, you'll know we only want what's best for us. For the human race."

"How will keeping us here help the human race? What could we possibly offer? You have a hundred times more guns than we do." My ability to speak was stunted by the image of the tied-up prisoners. I tried not to stutter or sound scared, failing miserably.

"You still don't get it. It's YOU. You're more precious than any gun you could offer. You and those damn fine ovaries. You three are at prime birthing age. That little one we can wait a couple more years on. But you three... you three will be put to work immediately."

"You want us to have *babies*?" Ashley spat out the words, her face twisting from doubt to unabashed anger.

"I want *us* to repopulate the great U-S-A. Before the radio went down, we were hearing the population worldwide was decreasing by twenty percent a day. I knew what needed to be done when I saw my first flesh-eater. Unfortunately, when we arrived at the base, it was clear that most airmen didn't get the bigger picture like us Marines. We'll deal with them, soon. As for those who understood my vision... well, they need to be content with their decision. And here you are... the ultimate prize." He looked at Cookie. "You'll serve a purpose, too, don't worry. Tony over there has a thing for Aretha Franklin. I'm sure we can find a way to put that fetish to good use." He smirked, then looked at Parker. "And you. I'm thinking we use you for bait. Even if those things get a few chunks out of you, you look like you have enough to go a few more rounds. Now, if you'll excuse me, I need to check on the others. Make sure they've finally settled down." He closed the door, before giving us one carefree wave.

"Oh, my fucking God, oh fucking A, what the FUCK is happening?" Bernice began breathing too deeply, her voice getting higher and higher. "I can't have a FUCKING baby! I just turned seventeen. I don't even know how to drive a stick shift! I've killed every plant I've ever owned!"

"Bernice. Shut up. Just hush." Cookie's voice sounded the way Celia's did when I gained more than a pound after the holidays. "I know what needs to be done. Just hush."

She took a deep breath. Turning to Monique, she lowered her arm to her granddaughter's mouth.

"Sugar, Imma need you to bite Nana real hard."

Monique's hair had gotten even whiter, her eyes as bloodshot as a junkie.

She had officially turned.

Monique let out a ravenous shriek, dripping drool.

She licked her lips before sinking her teeth into Cookie.

CHAPTER 16

"Cookie! Are you EFFING serious?" Ashley gasped, stumbling back into Bernice. "You just signed your death warrant. Hell, you just signed all of our death warrants!"

"Okay, honey, that's enough." Cookie winced as she wrangled her arm from Monique. "I *said* that's enough!" She yanked, and a bloody, bite-sized chunk of brown flesh tore off—an unspoken bribe for Monique to let go. Cookie kept her firm grasp on Monique with her uninjured arm, who, luckily, was too busy gnawing on a piece of her grandmother to struggle much.

"Um… this isn't a rabid animal bite that you can knock out with antibiotics. You are *literally* going to become a member of the undead. And like, we won't even know until you're eating us like a diabetic alone with a bag of caramels. Because you already have, you know… some white in your hair." I shrugged. "No offense."

Bernice rolled her eyes. "Don't be an ass. Obviously, Cookie did this to save us. So, she must have a plan."

We looked at Cookie expectantly.

"I'm playin' this one by ear, sugars. I'm sure I'll know when the sickness starts to take over. That'll be your cue to make a distraction of sorts." Cookie rummaged through her pocket, red liquid saturating her shirt's sleeve. She pulled out a set of keys and tossed them Parker's way. "Here. These are for you. The Caddy has enough gas to get you to the Alabama border and then some. What's left in the trunk should get you home. I know you were all worried about reading maps, but you'll be fine. I marked the roads and it ain't rocket science. The map is in the glovebox." Cookie paled with every word she spoke. She swayed, then plopped onto a cot. Monique yipped as she too was dragged toward the bed.

"Was it the bite? Do you think it hit a major vein or something? You don't look so hot." I pressed against a concrete wall, as far away from the infected duo as I could get, while still keeping Parker in sight.

"I think it's already happening. Lord, that was fast. My insides feel hot and my teeth ache like the dickens." A drop of sweat fell from her forehead to her collarbone. She shivered. "Oh, this feels *awful*."

Parker moved closer my way and brushed his hand against mine. He bent down so he could be eye level with Cookie, making sure to keep a distance from Monique's ivories. "Is it time? Are you ready for us to try and get out of here?"

Cookie watched Monique, who was staring at Bernice like she was a plate of chimichangas. A look of love passed over Cookie's face before she nodded. "It's time."

"How are we going to do this?" Parker asked, looking at me first. I opened my mouth, then closed it, shrugging my shoulders.

"Please, Kat. This is what you and I have worked toward our entire pageant lives." Ashley's eyes held shiny tears, but she didn't let them fall. She stood tall, and reached up to her hair, deconstructing her ponytail. Blonde cascaded down her back like she was the star of a shampoo commercial. She didn't have to tell me twice what the plan would be. I let my hair fall as well, running my fingers through the top to give it some volume. Ashley ripped the top of her tee so her cleavage would show. I slapped my cheeks for color and slicked my lips with gloss. I threw Ashley the tube and she did the same. We nodded at each other, silently approving the way the other looked. For good measure, I pinched my nipples so they would show through my shirt. Celia hadn't been above cheap tricks, and today, neither was I.

"Private! Excuse me, Private Harrison! We, er... we surrender, sir!" Ashley's voice was light, even a bit flirty. I worried it was a bit *too* much until Wes unlocked the door, walking in without his gun raised.

"Well, now isn't that the first good news I've heard in a while!" The private whistled as he looked Ashley over. "Beauty and brains! Your genes will make some great future patriots." He turned to me. "And you? You're on board?"

I let a shy smile cover my face. "Yes. I'm so sorry for before. I'm just... well. I've never you-know-what before. It took me by surprise. But I'm willing to do what needs to be done for our country." I lowered my head a bit, feigning embarrassment. In reality, it was so I could slightly roll my eyes without him seeing. If I wasn't so fond of the opposite sex I could almost entertain batting for the other team and see if Ashley and Bernice would show me the ropes. I couldn't believe the private was really falling for this. I always heard the world would be a stronger place if run by women. Gullible, beguiled Wes was Exhibit A.

The private was silent. Maybe I spoke too soon. Or maybe he had gotten a glimpse of Monique, who Cookie was basically sitting on to keep still.

"You. Come here." He spoke to me, beckoning with his finger. A small group of soldiers stood watching out the hallway window, all leering like chauvinistic bungholes. I didn't look at Parker as I slowly inched toward Wes. He grabbed me when I was in reach, pulling my face to his. "Convince me. Show me how much you want to stay here."

In my life, there were several times I had done things that I wasn't too proud of. When I was nine, I squirted eyedrops into a competitor's soda so she would have the runs, giving me a stronger chance at the winning title. At fourteen, I *may* have spread a rumor that our school's principal, a nasty woman who was always reprimanding me that my skirts were too short, was the *real* Zodiac Killer. As Wes's smooth lips made their journey to my glossy ones, I decided that getting ahead by acting dirty wasn't the way to go. Not anymore. Parker balled his hands into fists, and I motioned for him to back down. I snaked my fingers through the private's hair and as his breath quickened, so did mine. Just for different reasons. My hands found their way to a pair of ears which I locked onto, jerking my knee up into the private's privates. Before he could recover, I brought my other knee to his face, connecting nicely with his nose. Blood began to pour down his chin.

"Ow! You BITCH!" Wes doubled over and his gun fell to the ground. Parker dove after it as the soldiers that were standing outside came flooding inside. One shoved me aside, before looking past my shoulder. His mouth made a perfectly shaped "O." I turned to see Monique struggling to get out of her grandmother's grasp. Cookie, who was looking weaker by the minute, closed her eyes and let go. Monique shrieked gleefully and tackled Wes, licking the blood from his face as he tried to punch her off. The soldier closest to them brought his gun to her head, but he was too late. Cookie roared and opened her eyes—her red, bloodshot eyes. She flew at the man, her gaping mouth clamping down on his jugular. Blood sprayed onto the walls and onto the other now retreating and panicked soldiers. A loud gurgling came from the floor, where the once-handsome Private could no longer pass as a contestant for Mr. Universe. Monique crunched down on one hazel eyeball while digging through his chest cavity like it was a cereal box and there might be a prize at the bottom.

I didn't have time to gag. One of the retreating soldiers made a move to relock the door. Before I could stop him, Parker fired the gun, missing the soldier's head by a hair. They stared at each other. The soldier looked down at the door handle, then at the building exit. Cookie made the decision for him. Two hundred and fifty-plus pounds flew through the air like wires were pulling her from above. Her breasts smashed into the man's head first (classic Cookie with those honkers of hers), then her body into his, both of them toppling over like oak trees in dry season. His scream became a wheeze as his shaven throat disappeared under Cookie's mouth. She lifted her head, her body jolting in what looked like sheer bliss as smooth red plasma dripped down her chin. If there was ever an image to promote what horror looked like, this was it. Every fear I ever had (sharks, clowns, Celia) seemed trivial when staring at a woman covered in saliva and human matter.

"Go! We need to go, now!" Parker put his hand on the small of my back and pushed me ahead, Bernice and Ashley close behind.

A small figure blurred past us, blocking us from leaving. Monique sat on her haunches, head cocked as her red eyes narrowed in our direction.

"Nuh-uh. NO! WE. ARE. YOUR. FRIENDS!" I bellowed. Monique responded by slurping up a piece of slobber as she squinted hungrily at me.

Monique's eyes shifted and I held my breath, waiting to see some recognition. I was rewarded with a lip snarl. She kept her gaze on my greasy hairline and began to quiver. My body grew cold as I realized it as a telltale sign that she was about to pounce. I closed my eyes. This was it. This was the end. What a pity for any modeling agencies still left—they were about to lose an amazing future client.

Skin brushed by mine and I waited for the throat bite (from my experience these suckers really liked that area of the body). I heard a shriek. It took a couple of seconds to realize it didn't come from me.

I opened my eyes to see Monique viciously tearing apart a screeching dirty-blond twenty-something in camo. I noticed a large Chinese symbol tattooed on his upper arm, the ultimate telltale sign of a douchebag, and suddenly didn't feel bad at his demise.

"Come on! Let's go to the car!" Bernice shoved us into the hall, and Parker took the lead.

As we followed Parker into the hallway, soldiers shoved past us, not noticing us in their panic.

"Wait! The colonel!" Parker stopped and began to go back inside.

I wanted to argue, but I knew Parker was too good a person to let this go. "Argh! Okay, let's go. Hurry!"

Parker threw the keys at Bernice. "You and Ashley start the car. We'll be right there." He grabbed my hand and we rushed back into the hall. As we ran back, I caught a glimpse outside. Soldiers were running hysterically throughout the campus, monstered-freaks close at their heels. Rapid gunfire resonated throughout the base like firecrackers. It seemed Cookie and Monique had caused such a panic that the soldiers who were guarding the gate had left their post. There was now a giant hole in the gate we had driven through—like a bunch of somethings had chewed through to get to their food source.

Parker dragged me along until we were in front of the closed door that housed the bound soldiers. He looked around, before heading to one of Monique's victims. He kneeled and grabbed a hunting knife from the man's belt. He grasped it in his hands, took a quick breath, and opened the door.

The same man I had locked eyes with earlier gave me the same panicked look as before.

"It's okay. We're here to help." Parker panted, cutting the man's arm ties. He ripped off the gag, throwing it aside.

"Are you Parker? Parker Schroeder?" The man gasped, gulping in air. He rubbed his wrists.

"I am. Colonel Martinez?"

"That's me. I'll take it from here. You guys get out of here. Do you need a car? I'm sure we can spare a Hummer." The colonel got on his feet, looking powerful despite being in just his undies.

Parker handed him the knife. "We're covered with the car. We just want to get home. To Atlanta."

"Before we were ambushed by Private Harrison and his unit, we heard chatter of state line obstructions, mostly by civilians. I'd recommend going through Alabama on Highway 24, then 59 and get on 68. It's only a couple hours out of the way, maybe faster now that nobody cares about speed limits." The colonel bent to cut the ties of the soldier next to him.

"Twenty-four, fifty-nine, sixty-eight," I whispered to myself to remember the highway numbers when we got on the road.

"Thanks for that, Colonel. Can we help with what's happening here?" Parker vaguely waved toward the hall, which was now painted in blood splatter; the sound of heavy footsteps, high-pitched screams and sporadic gunfire surrounding us.

"We'll be fine. But I recommend you leave now." The colonel went back to freeing his comrades, dismissing us.

"You heard the man! Let's get to the car and get out of here." It was my time to grab Parker's hand and run.

We coughed our way through the smoky air, trying not to stumble over bodies—and trying not to pay attention to the ones that were convulsing.

Bernice had the car pulled up front. She threw open the passenger door, while Ashley held the backdoor open. We dove in and Bernice sped off. The SUV rocked as she drove over what remained of the front gate.

Were we finally going to be home today? Was Daddy even going to be alive? Would he even be happy to see me, after I told him Celia was dead? I couldn't help the questions that were flashing through my brain faster than Bernice was driving. I glanced at Parker, thinking of one more.

Are we still going to be an "us" when we get back to Atlanta?

CHAPTER 17

We found the first highway without issue. It was when we were halfway on the ramp that shit got real.

"Are those *grocery* carts?" Bernice slowed and we stared ahead at the jangled steel clump ahead of us.

"Worse than that. They look like they're carts from *Walmart*." I shuddered.

"We have to move them. They're literally blocking the entire road. This SUV's a beast, but I don't think it can handle ramming through that." Bernice came to a stop.

A knock on the driver's window made us jump. A scruffy kid, no older than ten or eleven, was pointing a gun at Bernice's head. He motioned for her to roll down the window.

"Jesus! Seriously?" Parker pulled me close to him, angrily shaking his head. His attitude distracted me from peeing my pants. Did he not see the gun aimed at his sister's forehead?

Bernice rolled her window down. From how freaked out she had been during the beginning of this whole stupid misadventure, she sure was handling herself like a champ. She stared coolly at the filthy boy who stared back at her just as unmoved.

"No grownups allowed." His voice was gruff as if he meant to try and intimidate us. It didn't work, even with the gun in his hand.

Through the windshield reflection, I could see Bernice's lips start to twitch. It was evident the rugrat saw it as well, and he clicked the safety off. Bernice's lip stilled.

"Where are your parents?" Ashley asked gently from the passenger seat.

"Probably digesting in a monster's stomach." Another boy, who looked to be only a couple years younger than us, had made his way to the window. He, too, carried a gun but his was the size of his body.

"Look, man, we're just trying to get home. We don't want trouble. Honest." Parker leaned forward to speak to the kids. He put his hands in the air.

"You got guns? Don't lie. The people before you lied to us. It didn't end great for them." The pre-teen kept his eyes on Parker, but his gun on Bernice and Ashley.

Parker was quiet for a couple seconds. "Yes. But I said we don't want trouble and we don't. We just want to go home. What can we do to get through?"

The older boy, obviously the leader, whistled. Boys of all ages popped up through the landscape like zits on a girl's face before school picture day. "Batman, keep the gun on them. The tribe needs to talk."

The little kid nodded seriously as his buddy disappeared by the side of the shopping carts.

"Batman?" Bernice asked.

"Dale—I mean Terminator, said we could choose new names."

"And you just follow... Terminator?" Ashley's voice was still soft.

"We're a family now." His chin wobbled. "Don't have any other left."

Another whistle pierced the air. Batman looked toward the sound. He nodded and lowered his weapon.

"Okay, get out of the car. And no funny stuff. If Terminator sees you sneaking guns and stuff he'll do something bad. Don't be dumb." Batman stepped back, waiting for us to open the door.

"Are we *seriously* considering getting out of the car? They could totally kill us! Let's just gun it and try to get through the carts." I hissed, keeping my voice low.

"The SUV wouldn't get an inch in that mess before Terminator decides to unload his AK-47 on us," said Parker. "We're taking a chance, I know, by getting out. But we're screwed. We don't have a choice."

I knew he was right. He had made the Varsity Debate Team when he was a freshman. I wasn't going to counter.

Ashley was the first to open the door. Bernice was a quick second when she saw her lover outside. Parker held my hand, and we climbed out together.

Terminator sauntered over like he was a grown man and not a child who had yet to see armpit hair. "Okay. We'll let you through. But we want all your weapons."

Parker stepped in front, shielding me. "Not going to happen. You're setting us up to die if we don't have anything to defend ourselves with."

Terminator made a face—a face I imagined he made when forced to eat his veggies. He crossed his arms. "Half.

That's my final offer. But if you take it, we want something else."

"What would that be?" Parker puffed his chest.

"A kiss. From each girl. A kiss for each guy here." Terminator's ears turned pink. The other boys giggled at each other. One threw a wink my way when he saw my expression.

"Absolutely not!" Parker was more outraged than when he was asked to give up our guns. My heart skipped a beat watching his red hair shake with disbelief. I'd never had anyone stand up for me like that before. I felt a stirring in the bottom of my stomach when I imagined how I could reward his bravery.

"Okay, fine! Ladies, wet your lips and let's get this over with." Ashley turned to Parker. "You're a sweetheart, but it's our decision. And I say it's cool. Bernice, you agree? Kat?"

Bernice looked visibly pissed, but after a short delay, she nodded.

"Kat?"

I wanted to be offended, but the last few days had been so awful that a few kisses meant squat to me. We were so close to being home that the thought of giving some quick smooches was a breeze. "Yup, I'm in." I, too, turned to Parker. "It means nothing. It's just a kiss."

Parker stepped my way. "Of course, it's your decision. But I don't think I'd be able to stand knowing some pipsqueak got a kiss from you before I did." He stepped closer and slipped his arm around my waist. He pulled me to him, and I melted as our lips met. His lips tasted sweet, like minty toothpaste, and he used just enough tongue to make me want more. We pulled apart, staring at each other with goofy grins on our faces.

"Well, that was a boner killer. You couldn't have waited?" Terminator huffed, showing his displeasure.

"Wish I could say I was sorry, but that was a long time coming," said Parker, smiling largely. "At least for me."

"All right, enough you guys. Our turn!" Terminator puckered his lips.

Ashley straightened her shoulders and walked to Terminator. She grabbed the sides of his face and planted a hard kiss on his lips. She let go and walked to the next kid to do the same. Bernice shuddered slightly and followed suit. I gave Parker one more lingering look before moving to Terminator, giving him a sloppy lip smacker.

When we were finished, each boy had a dreamy look about him. Batman was the color of a fire hydrant and looked to be on the verge of passing out from either excitement or embarrassment.

"Okay, you held up part one. Now the weapons." Terminator said, unable to look at us girls without flushing. "Lego and SpongeBob, you guys go with—wait, what's your name?"

"Parker."

"You guys go with Parker to get guns and whatever else we can use."

Two boys whose ages probably added up to less than mine, walked closely behind Parker as he opened the back of the Cadillac. I heard Parker raise his voice, and imagined one of them was trying to take his beloved hatchet. They walked back to us, the boys carrying four guns, ninja stars and a couple knives. I was happy to see the hatchet wasn't among the seized items.

"We're good here, Terminator. He even gave us extra ammo!" Lego grinned as he waved the bounty in the air.

"We keep our promises. We'll let you go, but we better not see you here again." Terminator gave one quick longing look toward Ashley before walking to the side of the stacked carts.

We hurried into the SUV before they could change their minds.

The boys began deconstructing the carts until enough were to one side that we could pass through. Bernice started the engine and slowly eased forward until we were on the other side. She slammed on the gas pedal, and soon, the lost boys of the highway were behind us. I tried not to think of the tears falling down Batman's face as we flew past.

Chapter 18

"Depending on if we have any more roadblocks, we'll either be in Atlanta in four-ish hours or... I don't know... another half-week or so." Parker held the map on his lap, tracing new lines to get us to Alabama, then from Alabama back home. "So, as much as it would suck to stop again, I think we should get provisions. We have lots of stuff left from Cookie, but I don't know how long we can make it last."

My stomach dropped. "Do you think it could really take that long to get back?"

"I hope not. But we don't know what's ahead. Don't worry, okay? We're almost there. I bet we'll be home without anything else happening." He pulled me closer and squeezed my hand.

"I say we drive until we near run out of gas." Bernice said over her shoulder. "Then we can try and find a store, get food and fill up the car with a can from the back. Okay with everyone?"

Parker voiced his yes, and Ashley and I followed suit. Bernice accelerated, only slowing down to get around abandoned cars. Cookie's SUV took a beating as it shoveled its way between cars too tightly stuck to swerve around.

We drove for more than an hour, just past a sign welcoming us into Alabama, before the Caddy's gas light blinked.

"The exit shows a Piggly Wiggly ahead. Let's pull over and see how it looks." Bernice said, reducing the car's speed.

"What if there's too many monster freaks? I mean there's only four of us now. And half the weapons. Do we really need food that bad? And don't you think all these stores will be wiped out of stuff?" Ashley's voice was shaky. I'm glad she asked because that too was weighing on my mind. I knew Ashley and I could survive without eating for a couple days. Hell, we'd been practicing for something like this since our first pageant. But Bernice and Parker were another story.

"It's not just food. I'm exhausted. I need something to keep me up." Parker yawned loudly. "Who knows when we'll get the chance to find a safe place to sleep again?"

I brightened. "You're with the right people if you need something to keep you awake!"

Ashley turned around and caught my eye. She gave a small smile. Up front, Bernice laughed knowingly.

"What do you mean?" Parker looked at me warily like I was going to pull out heroin and stick him with a dirty needle.

"Pageant crack! I doubt Pixy Stix were high on anyone's grocery list. We just need a dozen or so, and a soda. Or better yet, an energy drink. Mix those together and wowzah! You won't need sleep for at least two days." My heart quickened at the memory of drinking the "juice" before each pageant. Each mom had her own way of making it for their dolled-up kids. Celia took two parts Pixy Stix, one packet of raw sugar, one packet of honey, one Red Bull and a can of Big Red soda. As I grew older, I needed it less but my filled cavities were constant reminders that there were legal ways to stay awake.

"You guys are the experts. Sounds like it's just what we need. As for getting past flesh-eaters... well, in the movies they cover themselves with the guts of the infected. It's supposed to mask the 'alive' smell we have on us now. We could try it, you know. See if it works?"

"Hmm. Just to get this straight, you don't know for sure it will work. But because you saw it on TV, you want to throw insides on us on a Hollywood chance it *might* fool those things into not trying to eat us?" Ashley turned, her eyebrow raised. "I've been without deodorant for two days and I've been using my own spit as hairspray. If I have one more smell on me I'll lose my mind. Like, honestly, I will go totally batshit on y'all."

"So... no guts?" Parker asked, grinning.

"I'll take my chances." Ashley flipped back around.

"Ditto for moi." I wrinkled my nose. I had a weird thing about textures. I gagged every time I saw someone eating oatmeal. I couldn't imagine how I would deal having intestines draped around my neck like a wet feather boa.

Bernice turned onto the exit and drove until we found the store. She pulled to the front of the doors, turning the engine off.

"I say we put the gas in first. We don't know what's in there or how fast we might need to leave," Parker said. "We have enough guns and knives for each person to bring at least one weapon in. I'll go out first and start filling."

"Aye, aye, sir." Bernice found the gas tank button and opened the lid for her brother. Parker jumped out, grabbed a can and began filling up. I headed to the back with the girls, and we rummaged through what was left of the weapons. I saw a flash of white and pulled my pearl-handled gun from the small pile. I was hoping I wouldn't have to use it, but it gave me some comfort as the cold metal rested against the inside of my hand.

"Okay, all done. Ready to go inside?" Parker wiped his hands, leaving behind oily residue on his Levi's.

I handed him his beloved hatchet, and my heart fluttered when our hands touched with the exchange. It blew my mind that the guy I had marked off as a loser was making me feel like this. It sucked that it had taken a world apocalypse to make me see how great and kind he was. Even his rosacea was cute. Like a blushing, sturdy lumberjack.

We huddled together—Parker took the lead, I was second, and Bernice and Ashley brought up the rear. Though I knew what we could expect, it didn't make it any less frightening. Our breathing grew louder as Parker pushed open the door.

Up front, the checkout stands were torn apart. Cash registers were smashed beyond recognition. Light fixtures were dangling dangerously, giving off shadows of nooses swaying in an invisible wind.

"Well… this is encouraging." Bernice moved closer to Ashley. "It doesn't feel like I'm in *Friday the 13th* at all."

"Mama!" A child's voice echoed through the aisles.

"Did y'all hear that?" A scream I could have dealt with. A kid was another story.

"It sounds like it came from over there." Parker pointed his hatchet toward the Cleaning Supplies aisle. "C'mon!"

"No way! Uh-uh. It could be, like, a trap. How the heck could a kid survive this long alone?" I shook my head.

"But how do we know it isn't just one kid? A kid that's scared and all alone? Kat, I could never live with myself if we just walked away. I'll go alone if I have to." Parker began walking toward the sound, letting go of my hand.

I knew I had disappointed him. Ugh... why did I have to fall for such a good guy? I knew I couldn't let him go solo. "Hold up, I'm going with you."

The four of us crept as silently as possible past ripped bags of rice and crushed produce. We reached the aisle, and Parker peeked around the corner.

"Shit! Kat was right, it isn't just a kid. It looks like a lady and a baby in a stroller." He whispered. "I still say we check if they need help."

"Whatever. Just promise me that if anything seems off we run back to the car. Deal?" I was already pissed we had listened to Parker. I had a limit on being a good Samaritan and I was quickly reaching it.

"Deal." Parker took a step so he would be visible to the mom and child. "Excuse me? Ma'am? Don't be scared, we're here to help if you need it."

The rest of us crowded behind Parker, all of us clutching our weapons for easy use. The woman stiffened. She slowly turned to face us.

"Oh, good Lord!" Ashley threw her hand over her mouth, gagging.

The thing we had mistaken for a woman stared at us behind stringy, blood-soaked hair. Her jaw was crumpled like a recycled soda can, her throat half ripped away. Empty sockets met us where eyes should have been. Her mouth opened wide as she took a blind step our way before jerking back, seemingly not feeling the broken leg bone popping in and out of her thigh.

"Mama!" The same child's voice rang out again.

The woman tried lurching toward us again, but fell back in place like before.

"Shit on a yellow stoned brick road... look at that." Bernice pointed at the massive hole in the thing's stomach. Through the hole, I could see parts of the creature's spine that weren't hidden by tattered entrails. A string was wrapped around part of her exposed skeleton, the loose end tied to something in the stroller.

"Did she eat her *baby*?" Ashley clutched her fists to her stomach.

"Would it really surprise you at this point if it did?" I clutched Parker's fingers and we intertwined our shaky, clammy hands.

The thing turned, clawing at the string. While it was distracted, Parker grabbed a bottle of light soy sauce and threw it at the freak's head. The monster roared as the hard glass smashed against what looked to be a once-pleasant face. The blow was enough to shatter the glass into shards of confetti, except for one large piece that had broken off inside the thing's forehead. It faced us, its obviously un-Botoxed forehead furrowing in anger. The wound began to open and coagulated blood began clumping over dented cheekbones. It gave one last feeble screech before falling to its knees, then falling completely over. The end shards of the glass poked through the top part of the creature's noggin. If there was ever a sign that this mother-effer was kaput, this was it.

Parker was the first to take a step forward. When he saw me following he seemed to grow courage and took longer steps until he reached the figure on the floor. He nudged its head, relaxing when it didn't move. He looked at me, then peered into the stroller.

"Wow..." Parker reached into the baby carriage, grimacing as he felt around.

"God, be careful, idiot," Bernice said as only siblings can do.

There was more rummaging, then Parker held his hand up. In it was a baby doll. Parker pulled the string, which lifted the foot of the dead thing on the ground.

"Mama!" The doll called out.

"Are you kidding me?" Bernice let out a giggle. "It wasn't a baby! It's just a stupid piece of plastic."

A crash behind me made us all turn.

"Oops. Sorry." Ashley said sheepishly, picking up cans of lima beans she had knocked over.

Her head was to the ground, making it impossible to see the once-hidden zombie as it flung itself toward her body. Ashley fell forward, screaming as she hit the floor.

"Noooo!" Bernice shoved me into a shelf as she ran past to get to her beloved.

It was too late. The monster's mouth was already clamped down on Ashley's calf, salivating as it began to feast.

CHAPTER 19

"**B**ernice, get back!" Parker yelled as his sister began beating the sin out of Ashley's attacker. Bernice was shrieking so loudly she couldn't have heard him even if she was in the frame of mind to listen to directions.

"Arrrrgh!" With the strength of a CrossFit addict, Bernice hooked her fingers into the monster's eye sockets and ripped upward. The top half of its skull pulled back like a loose orange peel, Jackson Pollock-ing spilling brain and clotted blood onto the floor. Its semi-headless body spazzed for a few seconds before growing still.

"I'm going to die. Wow. This is it. I'm going to die in a mother fucking Piggly Wiggly. I didn't even get the chance to tell my parents off for the last time." Ashley was calm as she stared ahead at nothing.

"No, baby, no you aren't!" Bernice's voice shook as she held Ashley. She looked at her brother. "Do something!"

Parker's mouth opened, then closed, then opened again. "I don't... I don't know what..." He looked desperately my way.

"It's fine, you guys. Really. I'm not even that pissed." Ashley looked at Bernice. "Actually, I take that back. I'm SUPER mad at myself." She licked her lips. "If I had been true to myself a long-ass time ago I could have had more time being happy. I hid who I was for way too long."

Bernice began wailing even louder. Ashley absentmindedly patted her on the back, ironically consoling Bernice even though she was the one about to kick the bucket.

"Lovebug, stop crying." Ashley's voice was soft. "This could be a good thing. I'm having some major clarity right now. Look at me." She cupped Bernice's chin and lifted it so they were staring into each other's eyes. "Let me say what I need to say before…" She gulped. "Before it's too late." Her gaze turned to me.

"Kat. You are *so* beautiful." She smiled gently.

I smiled back. Well, at least she was lucid.

"But dear Jesus, inside you can be one of the ugliest people in the world."

Okay, not what I was expecting.

"I've known you for how long? Since we started competing at like, what? Two or three years old? And you've been an absolute bitch since day one." Ashley shook her head like she was disappointed.

"It's not like I had a choice." My defenses fly to attention. "Celia wouldn't let me have any friends. Especially girls whose parents let them eat gluten past six PM."

"Celia was a bitch, everyone knew it. I'm sorry you had to see her go so gruesomely like that, I am. But she was so awful. Do you know she tried to get me kicked out of the Miss Hardware Tools 'N Such pageant by saying I was 'potentially' having an affair with a judge? I was eleven."

It was pointless to argue, even if I had wanted to. Celia had introduced me to two things. One, how to prevent cellulite.

Two, that every female was to be avoided because they would try and bring me down any chance they could—and it was up to me to bring them down first.

"But you've changed. You really have. And hoo boy, no one was more surprised than me! I honestly thought you were a lost cause. You were just a soulless creature in that bananas body I could never get no matter how long I held a plank. And you've changed because you're finally finding out who you are. It's a great thing to see. It's also because of Parker. Him being in love with you was the worst-kept secret in Atlanta. Hell, Bernice told me he's loved you since we weren't but kindergarteners."

My face warmed as I sneaked a peek at Parker. Suddenly, Ashley's harsh words didn't matter much.

"Thanks a lot, Bernice," Parker muttered, running his hands through his hair.

"Oh, don't blame your sister." Ashley continued to speak tranquilly. "This is what I'm talking about. Life is too short. We need to be *honest* with each other. One day you're in the bean aisle of a grocery store, next you're a chew toy for some almost-dead once-human thing. My last wish is for us to just be truthful."

Bernice let out a strangled cry and clutched Ashley's arm, pulling her in. Ashley turned and shoved Bernice away.

"No! No kissing! You could get infected by me!" Ashley scrambled backwards. "We shouldn't be by each other. If my blood gets on you it could get in a cut or something. I would die all over again if I knew I made you sick."

We sat in silence and for the first time in my life, I didn't have anything to say. I looked at Ashley and her ruined leg. I did a double take.

"Ashley! Your leg!" I pointed, my face brightening.

"Well, don't rub it in, you jerk. I just gave you a whole speech about how you aren't so bad after all. Geez, maybe I was wrong and you really are—"

"Will you shut up? I'm trying to say your leg isn't bleeding. Maybe those cheap jeans acted like metal or something. Bernice, pull her pant leg up!"

Bernice had the jeans pushed up before I could finish my sentence.

"I can't believe it... Ash, it's just a bruise!" Bernice moved her hands over the darkened skin. "Zero puncture! No infection!"

"What?" Ashley stopped speaking in her freakishly still voice. "Wait, how? I felt the thing on me. It had a death clamp on my leg."

Parker looked around and spotted a packet of chopsticks hanging from an end cap. He grabbed it, tore it open with his teeth and fished out a pair. He went to what remained of the monster's head that was still connected to the body and squatted. Then he took the chopsticks and inserted them into the thing's mouth, prying it open.

"No teeth. Like, not even one." Parker looked at the body. "Hm... it's wearing overalls. That and no teeth..." He looked up to us, shaking his head. "Holy shit. Ashley, you lucked out big time. Looks like you were attacked by a redneck zombie. I thought I could smell moonshine on the sucker."

Ashley bent over, laughing as Bernice started sobbing, hugging her tight.

"Baby, you're going to be okay. You're going to be fine." Bernice said, furiously wiping snot from her nose. "Lord, I never thought I would say this, but I frickin love Alabama!

Where else could we find a frickin redneck zombie! And Ashley, I LOVE you. Good *God*, I love you."

Ashley took Bernice's face in her hands and gave her such a passionate kiss I felt like I was watching HBO. Turning away, I was surprised to feel tears slip down my face. I'd been experiencing more emotions in the last couple of days than I had my whole life. Folks I once counted as enemies, losers, and wastes of time were now the most important people I had in my life. I looked at Parker and saw him watching me with such a look on his face it took my breath away. I had never been in love before, but I knew this is what falling for someone felt like. My palms were hot, my heart was beating extra fast, and there was a constant struggle in my lower stomach that felt like I had eaten a box of worm bait and they were still alive, fighting to escape.

"We should go. Maybe we can grab some stuff on the way out. I just want to get back to Atlanta. Who knows what's there, if it's even still standing. But we need to find out." Ashley gave Bernice one last kiss, then stood up, rolling her pant leg back down. She helped Bernice up and I surprised myself by walking to Ashley and throwing my arms around her. She froze, then hugged me back.

If Celia could only see me now.

"Ooh! Red Bull!" Bernice said, holding up a large aluminum can in triumph. "This should keep us awake a bit longer. Enough to get us back home at least."

"Good job, babe!" Ashley beamed. "Okay, now let's get going. Come on, we're so close!"

Parker held my hand as we walked our way out of the store. If I squinted hard enough, I could imagine that he and I were just a normal couple shopping at Target for stuff we didn't need. If it wasn't for the obvious disarrayed state of the aisles and the smeared blood on Parker's shirt, it could have been a regular Sunday afternoon.

We got into the car, throwing the random stuff we had gathered into the back (Cheetos, a couple liters of off-brand soda, a box of crumbled cereal and a jar of pitted Kalamata olives). Bernice locked the doors and started the SUV.

"Okay, guys. This is it. Final stretch. I think we should go to the CDC first, but Kat, your dad... well... do you want to go to your place first?" Bernice turned to look my way.

"Um..." I looked at the faces watching me. Parker and Bernice's dad was at the CDC, probably the safest place we could go. Ashley's family wasn't even home. I knew the right thing to do was to not be selfish. I had come so far, physically and emotionally. But Jesus, I wanted to see my dad. He was a weenie, but he was a weenie who loved me, with or without Celia.

"We're going to her house. Dad's after." Parker spoke for me. I had been with the guy for less than a week and he already knew me. The feeling in my stomach got stronger.

Bernice drove off after consulting Cookie's map. Ashley tried to get a radio signal but again, we were met with static.

We sped like Highway Patrol no longer existed. Past turned-over cars and burning buildings and avoiding ravaged bodies like speed bumps. Ashley was the first to see the sign for Atlanta.

"We're here! Oh, my fucking God, we're fucking here!" Ashley gave a yelp, and her winning pageant smile that only came out for big events flew across her face.

A crashed helicopter and a fiery ambulance were the only detours we encountered before making our way into the city.

The car suddenly slowed, then came to a full stop.

"What's going on?" Parker asked. "We aren't there yet."

Bernice put her hands in her lap. She didn't turn around.

"I have something to say. I know we're close. But I... I need to get something off my chest. It's something I should have said a long time ago." Bernice coughed. "I don't know if I would have actually. But Ashley said something important. We should be truthful. And she's right. We've been through too much." She took a deep breath. "So, here it is. It was me." She looked down and whispered, "All of this is my fault. I'm the one who made this happen." She looked at me. "Celia is dead and it's my fault."

CHAPTER 20

"That isn't possible. What are you even talking about?" Parker grew still, his shoulders stiff as he stared at the back of his sister's head.

Bernice sniffed, her trembling hand noticeable from the back seat. "I didn't mean for this to happen. Not like this. I *swear*, I didn't mean to." She kept her head straight ahead, not looking at any of us. "Beaumont was supposed to be my last pageant. Hell, I only did them to add an extra-curricular for college. Dad always said I needed something more than just math league. And we all know I wasn't going to choose a sport. But God, pageants were just *awful*. From day one, I knew I wasn't going to fit in, but I didn't know how mean people could be. The girls... you wouldn't believe the stuff they would say about me. Even to my face."

My face flushed. I knew she was talking about me.

"The judges were worse." Bernice continued, softly. "I wouldn't even get pity points. They just gave me the lowest score possible to get me off stage. I wanted to quit *so* badly but I was still interviewing for colleges and, Sarah Lawrence, my number one, loved the fact that I had this crazy unique portfolio. Of course, toward the end it helped that I had Ashley.

I just needed one last pageant under my belt." Bernice gave a small look to the right.

Ashley was just as stoic as Parker. She didn't make a move to comfort her lady.

Bernice wiped her nose with her arm. "I tried to let it go. But I wanted to give the pageant a little scare. A memory I could take with me that would maybe ease some of the bitterness I felt for all those years. So, I went to visit Dad at his office. And when I left, there was a cart of mice just sitting there, calling my name. Okay, okay," she rushed, "I knew I was in a restricted area, and only there because of Dad's clearance. But his stories are so boring, I didn't think these mice could be anything more than missing a liver or something. I emptied the cage of like, I don't know, fifteen mice into my backpack. When I came home, I put them in an empty cardboard box— don't know how I didn't get bit—and brought them to the pageant." Bernice picked at her nails. "When I got there and saw Ashley, I knew I didn't want to go through with it. I was already having second thoughts on the way to Texas. So, the night before the pageant I decided to just forget the plan. I would bring them back to Atlanta and somehow get them back to the CDC. I mean, stuff must go missing there all the time, right? But when I went to feed the little guys some leftover room service, they were gone. A huge chunk of cardboard was missing from the side. Now that I'm talking about it, it was way more aggressive of a bite than I think mice normally take. They were all gone. I only freaked because I knew I was totally fooling myself by thinking my dad and his workplace wouldn't find out. I mean, yeah, they're busy, but there're cameras, like, everywhere. I didn't even think about where the mice went. I figured they'd find themselves outside and live a happy life away from prodding needles. It was only after we talked to Dad that I realized I fucked up. Fucked up big time. I had no idea..." Bernice swallowed loudly. She turned to me. "I'm so sorry. Your stepmom died because of me. Because I was an idiot and wasn't thinking. I don't know if you'll ever forgive me, but I'll spend the rest of my li—"

My punch connected with her nose before she could finish. I heard a ringing in my ears and my knuckles pulsed, letting me know I hit her square in the face.

"Owwww!" Bernice held her now-bleeding nose. "*Shit*, that hurt!"

"Kat, what the hell!" Parker reached into the back and grabbed the shirt I had gifted Ashley with in what seemed an eternity ago. He scrambled to the front of the SUV and held it against his sister's nose.

The happy-go-lucky feelings were gone. Instead, a white-hot anger throbbed throughout my body. My throat began to constrict as I struggled for air.

"Are you KIDDING me?" I panted. "You're defending *her*? The person who just admitted to ruining our LIVES? Who basically ruined the lives of every human being on EARTH?"

"Hey now, Bernice did a *really* messed up thing. But she didn't mean for this to happen. I think we just need to talk this out." Ashley broke her tensed posture to turn my way.

I couldn't stop the laughter that poured out of my mouth like water rushing from a broken dam. "Ashley, your family is most likely DEAD. Murdered actually. Basically, murdered by the person right by you. You're literally defending a MURDERER."

"Okay, that's enough, Kat. Ashley's right. You know my sister didn't mean for this to happen. We all make mistakes. I *know* she didn't mean it. How the hell could she have known?" Parker pleaded, looking at Bernice, then back to me.

"Parker's right," Ashley said. "You aren't so innocent. We *all* know you ditched us at the airport. Parker convinced us you weren't that bad and we should let you stay with us and to not say anything. But I saw you. I saw you look back at us as those monsters started eating everyone around us and I saw you look at the door and leave. But we're in this together and we'll only survive if we act like a team. We don't have time to linger on stuff that already happened. We have to move on."

I couldn't believe what I was hearing. I was in a car full of loonies. Bernice literally destroyed the world. And these two were acting like she had only admitted to stealing a pair of sunglasses. Who cared if I tried to save my own skin? They would have done it too if they'd had the chance. The point was that Celia was dead. And my dad might be dead too. But... there was a chance he was still alive. And I wasn't going to wait for my so-called companions to snap back to reality. I didn't need them. If I had my dad, we could survive on our own. We survived my mom leaving us, and I survived having Celia as a stepmother. We could survive this, just the two of us.

"I'm leaving. Don't follow me. I never want to see any of you ever again." I grabbed my pearled pistol. "If you try and come after me, I'll shoot you." I looked Parker in the eye. "Any one of you. I'll shoot you. Don't try me."

"Don't go! I'll leave instead! You'd be crazy to leave alone. Please... please don't go." Bernice dropped the bloody shirt from her face as fresh tears welled up in her eyes.

"I'm safer out there than in here with you," I said coldly, unclipping my seatbelt.

Parker placed a hand on my arm. I didn't look at him as I shook it off and opened the door. I began to run.

I didn't hear anyone following me.

Bernice hadn't parked that far from where we all lived, but I knew I couldn't openly head home in the wide streets. I was about six blocks away from my house, but I had jogged the sidewalks enough times to know there were lots of potential spaces for hungry monsters to hide in as they waited for their next meal.

I clutched my pistol as I passed by the Jensens' home, which was on fire; the Kirklands' garage, on which someone had spray-painted the words "ANNIE, DON'T COME IN. NOT SAFE"; and past the community park, which was full of half-eaten bodies. I remained alert, jumping at every noise and rustle I heard around me. I didn't know if it was a good or bad thing that it was so light out. I could see, yes, but that meant the flesh-eaters could see me too. I passed other houses, noticing that most doors had red biohazard tape wrapped around the doorknobs. It stopped when I reached my block.

I had crept along, stealthly but slowly, trying to not garner attention, but now that I could see my house and it wasn't in flames and looked as normal as could be, I couldn't control myself and sprinted ahead.

Standing in front of the door, I realized I didn't have my key. I reached for the knob, hoping it was open, and at the same time, hoping it was locked because that might mean my dad was inside, waiting safely for me. Waiting for me *and* Celia.

The door wasn't locked.

I slowly pushed it open, hating that my hands were quivering. It was hotter than a baked cow turd, but my body wasn't getting the message.

"Dad?" I cleared my throat and spoke a little bit louder. "Dad, it's me. I'm home."

Nothing but silence. I held the gun in front of me like in the movies as I moved around. A suitcase sat by the front door, and several pictures were missing from the wall. My spirits lifted as I realized that this meant my daddy had started packing. Maybe he was upstairs and couldn't hear me.

I started for the stairs, past the kitchen, then stopped. A bar stool was crooked. This wasn't anything so out of the ordinary, but my dad had severe OCD when it came to furniture placement. I walked over to it, then threw my hand to my mouth.

"Oh no oh no oh no oh no…"

An unnaturally large pool of dark red met me as I looked over the small kitchen island. Bloodied streaks in the same color smeared the cabinets, leaving a pattern that led to the backdoor. Two red hand prints painted the bottom of the door frame, a sign of a failed escape from whatever had dragged my dad outside.

I scanned the yard. No movement, no body. Just sunshine and a stack of wood waiting for winter.

Growing up, I thought my house seemed as big as the Disneyland castle. Now it felt small, as if it didn't have enough air. I dropped to the kitchen floor, staring outside. My gut was telling my brain that my dad was gone. Not just gone. He was dead. I should have felt sad. Maybe even angry. But I felt nothing. My brain was blank. If I closed my eyes, I knew I wouldn't wake up. I would slowly die, my body sinking into the hardwood floors. To never wake up again didn't sound so bad. Who would even miss me?

A creak behind me let me know that my time was coming up. Looking at my pistol, I realized I didn't have the energy to shoot anything. I didn't even have the energy to see what my executioner looked like. I just hoped the first bite wouldn't be too painful.

"Kat. Oh, Kat, I'm so sorry." Parker sat beside me and pulled me in to his chest. He stroked my hair as I sobbed loudly. I cried for time wasted and for memories lost. For Celia, for my dad, and for me. For my mom, wherever she went, and for my future. But more importantly, I cried for the present.

"I have no one. I'm all alone." I hiccupped as I tried to calm myself down.

"That's bullshit and you know it." Ashley sat down on my other side. She grabbed my hand. "You have us. We're your family. You're our family. We're in this together, forever and always."

The lost feeling in my toes and fingers slowly came back as I looked to Parker, then to Ashley. I saw a shadow and stiffened as I saw Bernice shuffling forward, watching me with a pained expression.

"I don't know what to say. If you want me gone, I'll leave. I swear it." Bernice's voice sounded funny. Probably because of her blood-clogged nose.

Parker squeezed my hand before I could speak. I kept silent for a minute or two as Bernice and I looked at each other.

"I'm sorry I was so horrible to you," I began, "that you felt you had to do something. I… I'd like to think I'm a different person now."

Bernice's face brightened with relief.

"But I can't forgive you. Not yet, anyways," I hurried, seeing Bernice's face fall. "Just give me some time, okay?"

Bernice gave a tiny nod. Parker squeezed my hand again. I rolled my eyes.

"And sorry I hit you. Not cool, I know."

Bernice shrugged. "Can't say I didn't deserve it."

Parker nudged me.

"Jesus! Okay, and sorry I left you all at the airport. I felt like shit about it and I'll never do anything like that again. Are we done?" I kept my eyebrow lifted as I glared at Parker. He smiled to let me know no more apologies were needed.

"Okay, guys, we should probably head to the twins' dad's office. It's kinda our last hope. And we're only a few minutes away." Ashley stood, offering her hand to me. I grabbed it and pulled myself up.

Parker kept his hand on my back as we walked out of the kitchen to the front door.

A large thump from above made us stop.

"I never looked upstairs! It could be my dad!" I headed for the stairs.

"No, wait! It could be one of those things. Just wait." Bernice blocked the stairway with her large frame.

I was going to shove past her, when at the top of the stairs, I saw the crouched shadow of a stance I had become too familiar with. As the thing crept down like a Japanese horror-movie villain, I realized I recognized who it had once been—Annie, the young daughter who lived just a couple blocks down— whose family had written the message on the garage door. Annie was no longer Annie. Her hair had been ripped out of her scalp, her clavicle visible through multiple bite marks and tears. She was in a soccer uniform, her cleats making clicking noises as she descended our way. She paused and sniffed the air violently before locking eyes with Bernice. Her fingers flexed in front of her, then she sprang our way.

I shoved Bernice out of the way and kicked Parker back. "Annie" fell on top of me and opened her mouth to expose an overbite and bits of flesh hanging from her blue and white braces. She lowered her head to my arm, biting into my skin, then my tendons and bone.

"AAAAAHHHH!" Flashes of light pounded through my head as I cried out in agony. I could feel every sharp-edged bracket around each of her canines as it dug deeper into my forearm. My free arm swung forward so my pearl-handled pistol was facing "Annie's" head. Her bloodshot eyes widened.

"Eat shit, bitch!" I screamed, pulling the trigger. My face was immediately splattered by brain and pieces of hard skull. I kept pulling the trigger until it clicked empty, then threw it aside.

Parker had his hatchet out, but stood unmoving, seemingly in shock. Ashley kicked the body off me—a soccer move I'm sure the real Annie would have been proud of.

"Kat... your arm..." Bernice's voice was shaking. "You saved me. Why did you push me out of the way? It would have gotten me, not you."

I clutched the bite mark, willing the pain that was getting worse by the second to stop. I grimaced. "I didn't want to see you get hurt. It isn't a big deal."

Ashley tore off a strip from the bottom of her shirt. She dropped to her knees.

"Let me tie this around your arm to stop the bleeding. I bet the CDC already has a cure. We just need to get us there."

I pushed Ashley away. "You don't know that. And you don't know how quickly I'll turn into... into that." I pointed to what was left of Annie. "You guys need to get out of here." I focused on a spot behind Ashley's head. I couldn't look at her or I would start crying again. "You saw how fast Monique and Cookie went."

"We can't leave you! We won't! Don't even say that." Bernice stood in front of me, shaking her head to make her point.

"You will. And you have to do it soon. I just have… I have a favor to ask. It's a big one." I had never been known for being brave, but I knew that what I was going to say had to be done. The sooner the better. "I can't become one of those things. Going around, eating people and all that nonsense. I need someone to… I need someone to kill me. I'd do it but I don't think I have the balls."

"Now you're acting crazy." Bernice's face was flushed and her eyes slanted in anger. "There's no way! You're going to be fine, we just need to get you to my dad's office—"

"I'll do it." Parker's voice was quiet, but it carried over Bernice's. "I understand. I'll be the one to do it."

I looked up, not able to hide the surprise on my face. That was fast. I thought I'd have to spend the next few minutes convincing one of them to get it over with.

Parker knelt next to me and put his forehead to mine. "Ashley was telling the truth, you know. I've been in love with you since we were both in our 'eating paste' phase." His voice cracked, and my face crumpled. I'd die from a broken heart if I didn't die from the virus.

"I don't want it to end like this." I felt tears gather and forced them down. "But it is what it is. I'm sorry you have to do this."

"I wish I had more time with you all." I blinked quickly as Ashley and Bernice began to cry. Turning to Parker, I gripped the stair's handrail for strength and took a deep breath. "I'm ready."

Parker shuddered, then stood. He hesitated, then grasped the hatchet with both hands.

He swung it high above his head, the blade glittering sharp through faded red.

I tightened my eyes so I wouldn't see him bring it down.

CHAPTER 21

ONE YEAR LATER

"C'mon, put some elbow grease into it!" Ashley yelped, then giggled as Bernice flicked her with water. The two had laundry duty this week, and since only the CDC was allowed to use the generator, electric appliances like washing machines were a thing of the past.

"It's nice to see your sister happy." Dr. Schroeder clasped his hand on Parker's shoulder. "I don't remember ever seeing her smile this much. And look at that sunrise. Have you ever seen anything so beautiful?"

"It's pretty nice." Parker looked wistfully at Bernice and Ashley and stopped shucking corn. Children ran around as families all over the camp began their day. For months, the remaining army had sent broadcast messages across Atlanta that there was a safe haven within the gates of the CDC campus. High walls topped with razors helped keep out the infected while keeping the hundreds of survivors safe.

"What's wrong, son?"

"Just wish Kat was here to see the sky." Parker cleared his throat, fiddling with a corn husk.

"I'm up, I'm up!" I said, sneaking up behind him before throwing my arm around his neck. "Wow, Doc, you're right, that sky is something else!"

Parker broke into a grin and turned around to greet me with a kiss. We'd been living together for a while now, and with everything we'd been through, morning breath wasn't something we worried about.

"Morning, lovely. I'll be right back with coffee. You want one?" Parker held up his empty mug.

I shook my head, smiling as I watched him walk away.

"It's also nice to see my son so happy. How's the arm?" Parker's dad stepped closer.

I lifted it out of my sling and held it out toward him. Or what was left of it. Turned out Parker had no intention of offing me. He knew there was a good chance of me surviving if he cut the infected arm off. He just didn't want to tell me in case I said no because a) I said it wouldn't work or b) the most likely reason—for vanity purposes. I had passed out after he chopped it off. Lucky for me, the group managed to get me to the CDC in record time, which thank the Lord, actually *was* a safe zone and free of zombies. The twins' dad managed to treat my arm, though it was touch-and-go for a while because of how much blood I had lost. But I survived, obvi. When I was finally well enough to leave the hospital room, Parker surprised me with one of my bright-pink beauty-queen sashes. I started using it as a sling right away, along with my new prosthetic arm which Parker had crafted by melting and soldering dozens of my tiaras. After about a month of living at the CDC, Parker and the girls had convinced a team of ex-SWAT guys to go on a rescue mission to my old home to collect the gear. Even though the doctor was pissed, he said he had never seen someone bounce back so quickly just because she had received shiny gifts. He totally didn't know me as well as his kids did.

"Looks like it's healing nicely. Just keep it out of the sun, use that ointment, and keep up with your arm exercises." Dr. Schroeder rubbed his neck. "I'll be in the lab most of the day. Bernice is coming in to help if you two want to stop in. We have a lot of cages that need washing."

Bernice had confessed to her father what she had done as soon as they saw each other. Because the CDC already knew the strain that had started the infection, they weren't too focused on how the virus had escaped, just on how to stop it. Dr. Schroeder knew that if the camp found out his daughter was at fault, the family, Ashley and I could be kicked out. It was a secret we would carry to our graves. That didn't mean that Bernice got off easy. She would be on trash duty until she was at least a hundred.

"Besides the arm, how else are you feeling?" Dr. Schroeder said quietly, his eyes glistening mischievously. He gave me a wink and I flushed. He hadn't been a big fan of mine when we first met. He had heard enough stories about me from Bernice to make even the most forgiving man upset. But he had gotten to know me, and through my charm and obvious love for his son, his opinion of me had changed. Especially since he and I had a secret of our own—that he would soon be a grandpa.

Happiness flooded my body as I watched my man walk back our way. I had held off long enough, and tonight was the night I would tell him our family was expanding. He was going to be a papa, and me, a mama. I would also tell him the sex of our baby. I knew it was a girl—I could feel it in my bones, right as rain.

I rubbed my belly, and smiled as I looked down.

"I think I'll name you Pageant."

ABOUT THE AUTHOR

S.L. Cunningham lives in Napa, CA where she owns an organic cactus water company. Her first novel, *Fauxcialite*, debuted in 2016.

Made in the
USA
Lexington, KY